CW00501142

THE O'MALLEY & SWIFT CRIME THRILLERS

Corn Dolls
Foxton Girls
We All Fall Down
The House of Secrets
The Uninvited Guest
Deadly Games

THE HOUSE OF SECRETS

AN O'MALLEY & SWIFT NOVEL

K.T. GALLOWAY

To S, thank you.

BLURB

The past does not sleep soundly.

Annie O'Malley has been signed off work and forced to take a holiday. With a lead on her missing sister, Annie travels north with DI Swift and together they rent a small cottage in the village where Mim was last spotted.

Only, the village has a dark history of its own.

The cottage was home to a family who haven't been seen in over forty years. Their things still packed away in the basement, awaiting their return. It's a macabre destination for the dark tourist, and the rest of the village isn't much more welcoming.

When Annie is awoken by strange noises, her belongings moved or missing, she tries to talk to the small community about what happened twenty years ago. But the villagers don't want to talk. In fact, they don't want Annie and Swift there at all.

As their aggression mounts, Annie wonders if the cottage is haunted by the ghosts of the family, or the secrets of the living?

The fourth in the best-selling O'Malley & Swift series; can Annie find her missing sister before the ghosts of the past awaken?

A NOTE FROM KT

Hi,

Thanks so much for picking up book four in the O'Malley & Swift series. I hope you're enjoying the series so far, and relish in hanging out with Annie and Joe. I'm so grateful to you for reading the series, as it means I get to write more!

It's great to be back, and this time in a different setting, up in the Yorkshire hills. As with all the O'Malley & Swift books, although the county may be real, the place names and people are definitely not.

So with no further ado, let's dive in...

PROLOGUE

CHLOE MANNING PEERED OUT FROM UNDER HER duvet into the darkness of the unfamiliar bedroom. Eyes watched her from every hidden corner; they peered from behind the curtains and blinked between the half-closed wardrobe doors. Though the night was cool, her little bed felt damp with sweat, her hair plastered to her neck and her forehead. She wiped it away from her eyes with the back of her hand. What had woken her? Was it the monsters waiting in the shadows?

"Mummy," she whispered, afraid if she talked any louder the monsters would peel away from the darkness and find her. "Mummy, please."

She looked around for Tommy Teddy, but he must had fallen out of her bed at some point in the night. *What if the monsters had taken him?* She shivered as her damp nightie stuck to her skin. The cupboard at the far end of the room ticked loudly, whirring to life, and Chloe ducked back under the blanket and started to cry. Maybe the monsters had gotten her mummy and daddy too? Maybe she was all alone in this weird cottage that she'd been dragged to in the school holidays when she'd much rather have stayed at home with the cat and the dog and all of her teddies.

The whirring got louder, pinching her head like when Mummy mixed all her fruits for breakfast in the blender. But this was scarier than that, louder, higher, it was the worst noise she'd ever heard, and it wouldn't stop.

Chloe ducked down further into her bed, her fingers pushed so hard into her ears that they ached. She felt around with her feet in case Tommy Teddy had been pushed to the bottom of the bed and was squashed between the mattress and the wall. He did that sometimes at home. If she could just find him, Chloe knew she would be safe. Her toes kicked out, bashing painfully against the faded wallpaper, cracking her nails so they caught on the duvet. Chloe cried out, the sound echoing around her blocked ears. She bit her lip, not wanting to draw attention to herself when there were monsters just outside the covers. Tommy Teddy wasn't there.

Chloe peeled a finger out of her ear, it popped with a pain that shot right through her teeth, but this time she was brave enough not to make a sound. She shuffled to the edge of the bed and lifted the cover just enough to see out from under it. The floorboards creaked with her movement, and Chloe could see dust floating through the shaft of light cast under her door.

"Mummy?" she whispered, wondering why her parents had turned the landing light on but not come in to see her.

The light swept across her floor catching the foot of Tommy Teddy as it disappeared. Chloe's eyes widened. She blinked, getting used to the darkness again, trying so hard to focus on where she'd seen her bear. He wasn't far, he must have fallen from the bed while she'd been asleep. If she could just reach out of the covers and grab him, she'd be okay.

Lifting the covers a little higher, Chloe stretched a bare arm out as far as it would go. Her fingers fumbled over the dusty floorboards, swiping across back and forth, the noise of her hands drowned out by the whirring from the cupboard.

That must be where the monsters live, Chloe thought, shifting her weight forward slightly so her fingers could stretch further. *As long as they're in the cupboard they can't get me.*

With that thought set bravely in her mind, Chloe moved her whole body to the edge of the bed and slipped down to the floor. The cupboard was at the other end of the room, the door firmly closed. Tommy

3

Teddy looked as though he was making a run for it as he lay sprawled on the floor, his head facing in the direction of the landing. Maybe Chloe could grab him and make a run for it. She could climb in-between her mummy and daddy where nothing bad could ever get to her. It didn't matter that she was nearly six, they'd make an exception this time. When there was something so scary in her bedroom cupboard, they couldn't send her away.

Chloe drew breath, kneeling up on the hard floor like a runner about to start a race, poised and ready to dash to Tommy Teddy and out of the room. The room around her moved with the whirring and the clicking and the rushing. Chloe tried to block it out again, whispering under her breath the song her mummy used to sing to her at bedtime.

Rock-a-bye baby, on the tree-top.

A gust of cold air blew around Chloe's bare feet and she shivered.

When the wind blows the cradle shall rock.

The curtains blew towards her into the room, flapping violently across her face. Chloe drew back, falling onto her bottom with a thud.

When the bough breaks the cradle will fall...

And down will come baby, cradle, and all.

4

Panic seized her whole body, she couldn't move, her lungs were paralysed and unable to draw breath, her legs and arms like marionettes without a puppet master. And so, when the noise in the cupboard juddered to a soupy silence that made Chloe's ears pop, she could do nothing except squeeze her eyes tightly closed.

There was no noise now, but the bedroom didn't feel still. A cold began to creep its way up from the floor-boards and around Chloe's ankles. It was unlike any coldness she had ever felt. Not the icy fingers of frost that made Chloe excited for sledging and snowmen, or the creamy coldness of ice cream and lollypops. This was a dull coldness that chilled through her skin all the way to her insides. Chloe's arms and legs prickled with goosebumps, but she kept her eyes tightly shut and didn't move back to her bed. She couldn't. The cold swept up her legs and blew around her middle, her nightie no match for what must be a breeze coming from her open window. But Chloe knew her window was shut. Her mummy had made sure of it before kissing her on the forehead and tucking her in. Tears loosened Chloe's eyes as she thought of her mummy now. How much she wished she was cuddling her and telling her it would all be okay.

The breeze moved up, tickling the back of her neck as though someone was there blowing into her hair. And it brought with it the smell of candyfloss. Sweet, cloying at the back of Chloe's throat with a sensation that she couldn't quite understand.

And then the room seemed to fall away from her. Sucked into a vacuum of stillness that made Chloe swallow quickly to try and hear past the silence. She felt like she was in a state of nothingness, and a fear swept through her so fiercely that she felt her head wobble too heavily on her neck.

It was too much. Chloe had to move. Despite her young age, she knew she was in danger. *Don't talk to strangers. Never take sweets from anyone you don't know. Always look twice both ways before crossing the road...* What was she to do in this situation? Hunted by monsters in a place that was supposed to be safe?

Run.

Filling her aching lungs with cool, sweet air, Chloe pushed up onto her haunches ready to flee. *Three, two, one...* She flung her eyes open, lifting up onto the balls of her feet and powering as fast as her legs would carry her towards the door and Tommy Teddy. But before she could reach either, Chloe's attention was grabbed hold of by something glowing over by the cupboard. She faltered, her vision blurred by tears, smudging the outline that was moving towards her as if floating on the freezing cold air swirling around her feet.

Chloe looked on, unbelieving, as a girl no older than she was, stretched her face into a smile and started to hum, her whole body glowing a soft blue that made her skin transparent. The smell of candyfloss grew stronger as the girl glided towards her.

It was as though her legs were no longer attached. Chloe dropped to the floor, clutching wildly for her bear as she fell, her bladder loosening and warming her legs. The room swam as an ear-piercing scream filled the air. Chloe shook her head back and forth, trying to stop it, trying to wake herself from this nightmare. And it was only as she felt consciousness slip away from underneath her, that Chloe realised the dreadful noise was coming from her own mouth.

ONE

Monday

ANNIE O'MALLEY SAT AS STILL AS SHE COULD IN THE passenger seat of DI Joe Swift's car. They were surrounded, the road was blocked in front and behind them, and low stone walls sat too close to the car doors to push them open and escape. What must be a dozen pairs of eyes stared at her through the windshield and, if she twisted her head and looked out the rear window, more were there too. Watching, waiting for her to make a move.

The heat from the late April sunshine, magnified through the glass on all sides was making Annie's bare legs stick to the leather seats. And a layer of nervous sweat wasn't helping matters. She shoved her hands under her thighs and peeled her skin away painfully from the seat, tugging her shorts to free them from where they'd bunched up at the top of her legs.

"What do you suggest we do now?" Annie whispered at Swift, trying not to make any sudden movements. "There's no way out."

Swift shrugged slowly just as the car started to rock from side to side, a teeth-aching scrape sounded from somewhere near the rear wheel arch.

"Swift!" Annie hissed, grabbing on to her seat as though she was about to be tipped out. "Do something."

"What do you suggest I do?" he hissed back; his own hands white-knuckled on the steering wheel. "I can't just drive through them."

The 4x4 gave a violent judder towards the stone wall on Annie's side. She squealed and pressed her hands to the window, not wanting the glass to cave in and shatter all over her face. The car rocked and landed back on all four wheels. But the let up was only momentary as they shunted forwards with small, but stomach clenching, movements.

The stench was awful, like warm meat and sewage, and it filtered in through the air system that had shut down with the engine.

"We'll have to just wait it out and hope for the best," Swift whispered, removing his feet from the pedals and yanking up the hand brake.

The car stopped its propulsion forwards, jerking both Annie and Swift towards the dash. Annie shuffled back, manoeuvring her feet up against the glove box, ignoring Swift's dagger-eyes. At least she'd taken her shoes off and wouldn't leave a mark, which was more than could be said for what was going on to the paint-work outside.

It was supposed to be a holiday. A week away in the Yorkshire Dales, to not only celebrate the end of Annie's recovery from the last year, but also to follow clues drip fed to her by a now-dead psychopath about Annie's missing sister, Mim. And now Annie and Swift were stuck about five miles out of their destination with no hope of rescue.

Using her techniques as a psychotherapist, Annie did a round of deep, relaxing breathing which resulted in nothing more than a swimming head and a build-up of panic. For a fleeting moment, she was glad she no longer worked as a psychotherapist, then remembered she was stuck in a car with the detective who'd lured her back to the police force and couldn't weigh up the better of the two. Or the worse.

A sharp, tooth-jangling squeal of metal drew Annie's attention to a large body trying to pass between

Swift's car door and the wall, taking the wing mirror with it.

"Argh," Swift yelled as quietly as he could. "Annie, I think it might be time to call in some backup. But I have no idea of the local force's number."

The car jolted to the side again and Annie couldn't help but scream, one hand flying out to brace on the side window, the other finding the side of Swift's head. He yielded much more than the glass, toppling to the side, bashing his head against his own window.

"Ow," he yelled. And with the noise of his skull hitting the glass, and the yell that accompanied it, all eyes were now on the interior of the car and not just its shiny paintwork.

Annie held her breath, fighting against the burning in her lungs. And when a sharp rap of knuckles hammered out on the rear windshield, she almost lost control of her faculties.

Both Annie and Swift spun in their seats to face the angry fist shake of a man dressed in a checked shirt and gilet.

"What're you doing?" the man yelled. "This is a private track. You're blocking the way of my herd."

The large Highland cow who, moments earlier, had taken off Swift's wing mirror turned to face them, it's expression almost as scary as that of the angry farmer.

The mirror hung jauntily from its horn. The farmer plucked it off, gripping the pole and brandished it like a weapon.

"How'm I s'posed to get this lot moved now?" he shouted.

Both Annie and Swift swung back around in the car. The herd of hairy cows on the road ahead looked in no hurry to move in any direction.

"What happened to *I'll map read, Swift, I'm a natural?*" Swift hissed, keying the car engine back to life.

Annie stifled a grin, not sure it'd be appreciated right at this moment in time, what with the damage to the mirror and the absolute certainty they weren't going to get out of this situation without more scratches to the paintwork.

"Sorry," she said instead, biting her lip.

Swift huffed out a sigh and wound down his window so the farmer could hear his reply. The smell of manure flooded the car so thickly now, Annie could feel it in her mouth.

"Sorry, mate," Swift said, jovially over the mooing. He was good at placating people when needed, it's what made him a great boss. "We're a bit lost."

He added a little denigrating laugh to his words, but the farmer looked unshaken by Swift's ocean blue eyes and beaming smile.

"Shall we reverse out?" Swift added, undeterred.

The farmer honked a laugh of his own. "And how do you propose getting past that, then?" He nodded his head behind him, and Annie twisted back around in her seat to peer past the dozen cows and their owner to a large, muddy tractor. "If you move very slowly forwards then they should bundle out of your way. Just don't run any over or I'll be sending you a bill. I've got your number plate written down so don't think I won't be able to find you."

"God forbid," Swift muttered, putting the car in drive and edging slowly forwards. "What about the damage to my paint work?"

Annie batted him gently with the back of her hand. "Just be thankful we're being allowed out at all. He might have kept us to feed to his pigs."

"Whose bloody idea was it to come on a holiday to Yorkshire, anyway?" Swift huffed, and Annie noticed he'd turned a slight pinkish hue. "Sorry, I wasn't thinking. My brain is too full of... beef."

The cows were caught in the headlights of the car as though mesmerised. Though it was only dusk, the bulbs shone brightly into their huge eyes, making them look almost rabid. They shouted at the car in protest but made no attempt at moving out of their way.

"It's okay," Annie said, lightly. "I'll add it to my list of things I owe you for."

Truth was, the list was long and growing longer by the day. When Annie had broken her ankle last year on only her second case, Swift had taken her in and looked after her. Her flat-cum-office was no place for a person with their leg in such a thick plaster it meant they couldn't weight bear. Then, during their last case together, Annie was sucked down a rabbit-hole by a man who only wanted to do her harm. Harry Metcalf, handsome GP but also crazed killer. Swift had been there for her just when she needed him, in a bathroom full of the dead-man's blood. Before Harry had succumbed to the lethal injection Annie had stuck in his neck, he'd teased her with the idea that he'd met her missing sister. A sister Annie hadn't seen since her father absconded with her nearly fourteen years ago. And with the name of a village and a rage in her heart Annie had organised this trip to try and track Mim down herself. Swift was only on the journey with her because he hadn't taken no for an answer.

"There are two bedrooms in that cottage you've booked," he'd said to her one morning in a cafe across from their offices. "It'll be good for me to get out the county, it's been a while."

Annie enjoyed spending time with Swift, he made her laugh, and smile, and he made her feel safe. So, even if she'd never admit that to her new friend, Annie was glad to have him along for the ride. Even if he was sighing with intent at an annoying frequency at the immobile cows.

"Shall I climb out the window and shoo them away?" Annie asked, when Swift started muttering under his breath.

He looked her up and down. "You know what? That's not a half-bad idea. Do you think you'll fit?"

Annie moved her head as though he'd just slapped her. "Er, enough of that, thanks. I'm svelte and lithe I'll have you know."

They both knew that was a lie, but Swift just grinned at her and placed his hand on the middle of the steering wheel.

"I wouldn't do that if I were you," Annie said, shucking down in her seat. "You never know what'll happen? Those horns could do a lot of damage. They might turn on us."

"And trample over the car?" Swift shrugged. "I'm willing to take that risk because a) I need a beer, and b) I need a wee and I don't know which one can wait the longest."

Swift pushed his thumb on the horn sending a squeaky, high-pitched beep into the valley.

"Not what I was expecting," Annie laughed, then stopped abruptly when the farmer gave an irate shout and the cows started scattering down the lane as fast as their hairy legs would carry them.

Their large bodies bounced off each other and the stone wall; if there hadn't been an angry farmer hammering on the rear window it would have been quite hilarious.

"Drive," Annie shouted, not knowing if Yorkshire farmers were as prone to carrying shotguns as Norfolk farmers were. But she wasn't in the mood to find out.

Swift set off down the lane after the cows. They veered off with remarkable fluidity between a gap in the stone wall where a gate was propped open by a young girl in wellies and a worn-out Barbour. She can't have been older than double figures, but she flipped Swift the bird as they drove past.

"Charming." Swift raised an eyebrow.

"You did drive down their private lane and beep your horn at their herd," Annie shrugged.

"*You* made me drive down a private lane," Swift squealed back. "Now where the bloody hell are we going?"

Annie looked down at the paper map on her lap, her only choice since her phone had died and the sat nav in Swift's car lay on the back seat as uncharged as it was when they set off. She lifted it up to eye level, turned it around a few times in her hands and put it back down again.

They were at a cross-roads, luscious green fields falling away all around them. It was a stunning backdrop but that didn't make them any less lost.

"I have absolutely no idea," she admitted.

Swift threw the car into reverse and grabbed hold of the back of Annie's chair. Driving faster than was recommended, Swift backed them all the way up to the feisty young girl and wound down Annie's window.

"Ask her where we're going?"

"Excuse, me," Annie said loudly as the young girl was leaning over the now closed gate. "We're lost. Please can you tell us the way to a village called Ethlake?"

TWO

THIRTY MINUTES AND A WHOLE LOT OF SWEAR WORDS later, Annie finally saw a sign announcing their arrival. Ethlake. It was a bit misleading as there was no lake, but from her extensive research of the small village, Annie knew it was named after a local historical family and not a body of water.

It felt quintessentially British. As though they'd just driven into an episode of Marple or Midsommer, though Annie hoped it would be without the added murders. Creamy stone cottages semi-circled around a large village green—replete with duck pond and family of ducks—and bordered on the other side with a line of trees leading to a thick wooded area. The bell tower of a large church watched over the green from behind the houses. The ornately decorated pinnacles reminded Annie of a crown.

A couple of families gathered on the green, laughing loudly as the children played together on the grass. The adults sat together on a pile of picnic blankets eating food from a wicker hamper.

"I feel like I've gone back in time to the fifties," Swift whispered, as though the people outside the car could hear him.

Annie knew what he meant. Even the groups of teenagers walking along the roads towards their car looked happy and carefree and not as though they were about to rob them at knifepoint which was Annie's default position when it came to anyone remotely young. Though, at thirty-five, Annie was old enough to know better.

Swift drove carefully around the teens, Ethlake's roads were too small for pavements, and pulled over in front of a village store with an old-fashioned ice-cream sign out front.

"I thought you were desperate for a wee?" Annie asked, eyebrow raised. "That was over half an hour ago now, did you give up and go on your seat?"

"Don't be gross," Swift said, climbing out of his side and stretching up to the sky with a groan. His bones clicked loudly enough for Annie to hear and want to join in. "We need milk and bread. And I need more beer than I brought with me."

Annie climbed out of the car onto the road and stretched herself up to the sky. It was a beautiful evening. The sun shone orange and pink, washing the clouds with colour right out of a painting, and reflecting on the cottages and the pond. It was idyllic. Annie closed her eyes and held her face skywards, feeling the last of the sun's heat on her skin.

"But now I've stood up I may pee myself right here and now." Swift broke her peace the way only he could.

Annie smiled and shook her head, blinking the pink spots from her eyes. They walked either side of the car and Swift held the shop door open for Annie, the little bell tinkling as he did. The inside was just as perfect as the outside. Rows of food led to a till area with jars of penny sweets lined on shelves behind a red-cheeked woman in a tabard.

"You get the milk and I'll get the humbugs," Annie said, not waiting for Swift to agree before heading up to the woman to introduce herself.

With a beaming smile on her face, the woman could have been early thirties or late fifties. Her skin was glowing, and her hair curled around her face like she'd had it in rollers all night and sprayed it with a can of hairspray to keep them in. But when she moved to greet Annie, her hair moved too, so Annie put it down to good genes instead.

"Hi," Annie gave a small wave. "We're here for a week's break. What a gorgeous place you live in."

The woman's cheeks grew redder with her smile. "We like to think so too," she said, her Yorkshire accent thick and homely. "You staying up at Crow Cottage?"

Annie nodded, her eyes drawn to the rhubarb and custards behind the woman's head. Boiled sweets in yellow and red filled a glass jar, making Annie's mouth water. She could almost taste their sweet tangy deliciousness.

"That's right," she said, tearing her eyes away, not wanting to seem rude. "Can't wait to get in and get the kettle on, I'm gasping for a cuppa. We've just stopped for provisions first."

The woman narrowed her eyes, tucking her hands into the giant pocket at the front of her tabard.

"You don't look like macabre tourists," she said, studying Annie's face. "You and your fella after a bit of ghost hunting, are you?"

"What? No," Annie replied, her nose crumpled. "He's not my fella."

The woman raised an eyebrow and nodded slowly. "Right you are. Shame. Shame."

She looked over at Swift appreciatively as he checked the use by date on a few loaves of bread before settling on one he'd grabbed from the back of the shelf. Annie rolled her eyes, used to women of all ages, and men too, admiring Swift's good looks, she went back to ogling the jars of sweets instead.

"Actually," Annie started, when the woman's attention waned. "The reason we're here is because I think my sister stayed here for a while?"

The woman's eyebrows lifted. "Ah, another ghost hunter. Did she recommend Crow Cottage to you?"

Swift sided up beside Annie, un-ladening his arms onto the counter.

"Not as a guest, no," Annie replied, dropping a couple of Double Deckers onto the pile. "She lived here in this village for a while. Maybe still does. Mim her name was, is... I haven't seen her for a few years so I'm trying to track her down. Do you know her?"

"Can't say I recognise the name." The woman's smiles were long gone as she flapped open a carrier bag and started scanning the milk, bread, and chocolate.

"She's a lot younger than me, only twenty-one," Annie pushed, the hope that had been ignited in her belly all the way up the A1 threatening to die out here before they'd even really set foot in the village.

"Nope," the shopkeeper replied, not looking at Annie. "I know all the folk here in the village and I can't say I know who you're talking about."

Annie's lip wobbled and the woman snatched a look at her.

"But hey," she added. "There's a lot of folks live here. And you've picked the best week to come visit us. It's coming up for the May Day celebrations. There's a lot of things planned for the weekend, and everyone will be out to enjoy it. Maybe someone else will know who you mean, love."

With a quick nod of her head, Annie took the proffered bag and left Swift to pay for it. She made her way past the full shelves and pulled open the door, the bell tinkling not so sweetly on the way out. Dropping the bag by the car, Annie figured it would be safe enough for a couple of minutes and crossed the deserted lane to the village green.

"Where are you, Mim?" she whispered to herself as her feet sank into the soft grass.

The green was filling up with what Annie assumed were villagers, the young and the old congregating together like one big family. It had a charm, and Annie could see why Mim would have found herself a home here. She was always the chatty one, the friendly one, the one who could hold a conversation without feeling self-conscious about what she was saying. But then she had only been three when Annie had last seen her and perhaps her confidence was the confidence that came with being so young. Not yet knowing what the world held in store for her.

The ducks were paddling across the pond so Annie walked over to the edge of the water to see them. There, by the top of the green, she could watch over the rest of the village without feeling too conspicuous. A party atmosphere drifted over, from the cheery voices to the children laughing, there was even a small group of women sitting in a circle singing what sounded like a cantillation. Their voices harmonising sent a chill of wonder down Annie's spine.

Just beyond the groups of people was an unlit bonfire. The wood stacked neatly as though someone had been trying to build a teepee, only the scruff of kindling, dried grass, and crates at the very bottom gave away its real purpose. And, down at the far end of the green was a simple pole stuck into the ground, striped red and white like the sweets in the shop jars. It was as tall as the bonfire, with strands of material tied tightly in a grand knot, waiting to be untied and wrapped neatly around the pole. *May Day celebrations* the woman in the shop had said. Annie hadn't really taken notice of the date when she'd booked the break, it was the first available week for the only rental cottage in the village when she'd looked a few months ago so she'd snapped it up and maxed out her credit card.

"This place is weird," Swift said, coming up behind Annie and making her jump. "Sorry. Here."

He shoved a small striped paper bag in her direction.

"Weird?" she questioned, untwisting the top and doing a little jig at the contents of yellow and red boiled sweets. "I think it's delightful. Look at all those happy people who quite obviously have their work life balance the right way round."

Swift made a non-committal humming noise and stuck his hand in the open bag, pulling out a sweet.

"The woman behind the till asked me to give you these as an apology," he told Annie as they started walking back towards the car. "Said she didn't mean to put a dampener on your search, and she hoped you'd find your sister."

Annie sucked hard on her sweet, loving the combination of sweet and tangy. Musing over what Swift had just said.

"Let's get to the cottage," she said, eventually. "I'm dying for a cuppa."

"Me too," Swift agreed, bleeping the car unlocked. "And I may or may not have weed in the freezer section of the village store, so let's never go back."

Annie burst out laughing, nearly swallowing her sweet whole. He always knew how to cheer her up.

"Oh, and did she tell you about where we're staying?" Swift said, putting the car in drive and making his way through the busier lane as more and more of the village made their way to the green.

Annie shook her head, taking another Rhubarb and Custard. "She probably did, but I'm afraid my mind was rather tunnelled on Mim, sorry. But I do know that it's just the other side of the church, so it's just around the green and up that road…"

"No, I know where I'm going," Swift interrupted, not unkindly. "I meant, did she mention what people think about the cottage?"

"Oh, sorry, no."

"That it's haunted by the family who used to live there."

"What?" Annie turned to Swift, the disbelief quite apparent in her voice.

"Yep," he continued, undeterred. "They went missing nearly forty years ago, around this time of year in nineteen eighty-four, and there have been numerous sightings of them over the years. It's why the village is on the map. Crow Cottage, the most haunted building in the North of England."

He passed his hand across the windshield as though those words were depicted there in lights.

"They went missing?" Annie asked, her interest piqued. "What happened to them?"

Swift shrugged. "I didn't have time to ask, as I saw you'd left our shopping on the road next to the car. But I'm sure we won't have to go far to find out."

Annie knew all about missing families, her own paving the way for many a late-night search through the internet. And she wondered, as they drove around behind the forbidding church tower, if this was the first clue she needed in her search of Ethlake for Mim.

THREE

CROW COTTAGE WAS TUCKED AWAY ON THE EDGE OF the village. With the bell tower and graveyard on one side and an old, dirty water tower on the other, it sat almost entirely in shadows. Swift whistled, as he pulled off the road and onto the gravel driveway at the front of the cottage.

"Hope that's not where our water is coming from," he said, stretching his neck to see to the top of the water tower through the windshield.

"That's got to have been decommissioned at least a decade ago," Annie replied, noticing the unfortunate amount of bird droppings stuck like a fancy iced cake on the circular rim. "At least I hope so."

"Good job I picked up more beer," Swift shrugged. "Now let's get inside so I can bagsy the best bedroom."

Annie pushed open her door and jumped down onto the driveway. It was littered with weeds and grass, the gravel poking through heroically in patches that were being slowly overcome. Leaving her bags in the car, she skipped across the drive to the bird shaped welly scraper and lifted it to retrieve the key the owner had left for them. Annie knew from the particulars that there was an en-suite double room and a child's single. And Swift may be doing her another favour coming with her on this search, but there was no way she was having a small bed when, back home, Swift lived in a giant house, and she slept on a pull out camp bed in her office.

She twisted the large iron key in the keyhole and felt the lock give-away under her fingers. Ducking through the low mantel, Annie found herself in a small porchway, a shoe rack and coat stand took up most of the space on the stone tiled floor. Further through was a cute living room with wood burner, comfortable looking sofas and a bookshelf filled with well-thumbed paper backs. Annie ignored the door through to the kitchen at the back of the cottage and started up the wooden staircase at the edge of the living room. Greeted by low, beamed ceilings and three wonky wooden doors, she picked the one at the front of the house and opened it to a small bedroom with a narrow window and a double bed. Another door led to the small en-suite but Annie bypassed it and went straight to the window, leaning her chin on the cool glass. The view was over the village green, if she squinted and angled her head to see between some more cottages. It was either that or she could check out the headstones in the graveyard that seemed to snake its way across the front of the cottage, enclosed by spiky iron railings held up with ivy.

The floor creaked and shifted beneath her feet as Swift climbed the stairs and walked across the small landing to his own room. Annie heard a sigh and went to look at his room. It was smaller than Swift's utility room back home. But the single bed looked comfortable and, with the cupboard in the corner, at least he had somewhere to store his clothes. Swift dropped his bag on the bed and went to investigate; he lifted the latch and they saw a great hulking water tank and no shelves.

"Isn't this lovely?" Annie said, clapping her hands together. "I'll go and get the kettle on. Bathroom's next door if you're still busting."

Swift raised an eyebrow but, to his credit, he smiled along with her enthusiasm.

"It's quaint," he said, edging past Annie to the bathroom. "Like this avocado suite is quaint."

He shut the door and Annie took leave down the stairs. The kitchen was small but perfectly formed. Wooden cupboards sat on top of the tiled floor, and Annie spotted the kettle plugged in near the sink, a small hamper beside it. The owners must have left them a welcome basket. There were teabags, individually wrapped biscuits, coffee, and a waffle tea towel that looked new. Annie filled the kettle and switched it to boil, checking out the cupboards while she waited. There were the usual pots and pans, white plates stacked among bowls and Pyrex. There was a small pantry cupboard with a few left-over cans of beans and tomatoes. Everything was spick and span, and the whole cottage smelt as fresh as spring blossoms.

The kettle clicked off and Annie poured water into two cups, dunking tea bags in as Swift ducked through the door. It was a small room for one person, and with Swift's bulk it felt rather cosy. He handed Annie the milk from a carrier bag in his hand and left the rest on the little two-person table against the only free wall. She took through their drinks and found him laid out on the larger of the two sofas.

"Here you go," she said, handing him over one of the cups.

He thanked her and she sat down opposite him on the sofa in the nook under the stairs.

"I don't know why, given that I barely knew her," Annie started, sipping her tea thankfully. "But I can see Mim in a cottage like this one. I bet she covered it in brightly coloured rugs and paintings like the ones Dad used to have. Mum got rid of those pretty soon after he ran off, she is very much a minimalist."

Annie stared out of the window to the ever-darkening sky, the oranges and pinks from the low sun shone in through the glass and bounced off the whitewashed walls like a kaleidoscope. She closed her eyes for a moment, enjoying the heat on her face.

"Does she know you're here?" Swift asked. "Your mum I mean."

The old familiar feeling of guilt flooded Annie's empty stomach and gurgled with the tea and acid already there. It wasn't that Annie hadn't wanted to tell her mum what she was planning, it was just finding the words to say it.

"Not yet, no," Annie replied, feeling a bit sick. "I thought I'd wait and see if I get any leads before I get Mum's hopes up, you know?"

It was the line she'd been telling herself, but now Annie was here in the village, it didn't feel enough.

"Truth is," Annie added, chewing on her bottom lip as she tried to work up the courage to be honest with Swift. "It's been a while since I spoke to Mum. We don't often talk anyway, and, you know, since Christmas I've been busy trying to track down the village and…"

The more she spoke, the more Annie knew her excuses were just that. Excuses.

"It's okay, O'Malley," Swift said, taking another gulp of hot tea. "You don't have to explain your relationship with your mum to me, not if you don't want. I figured stuff between you isn't great anyway, given the amount of time we've spent together this last year, and how little you've really spoken of her. But I get that whole complicated family dynamic, trust me, probably more than you know."

More than you'll talk about, Annie thought, remembering how Swift had kept it a secret when his own mum had come to stay. Every time Annie thought about it, Swift and she had more and more in common.

"Families, hey?" It was an annoying answer, but she gave it anyway. "I'll talk to Mum as soon as I find anything out. So, tell me more about this missing family that used to live here? I have to say, the place doesn't feel haunted."

"Wait 'til the sun sets and the darkness descends," Swift said. "There are no streetlights here and that always makes me a little nervous. Do we know if there are any torches or matches and candles around?"

"I'll finish this up and have a look."

Swift nodded. "But other than what I told you in the car, I'm not sure about what happened. I tried to Google it, but I'm going to need to find the wifi code because there is no 4G out here."

Annie gulped the last of her tea and slapped her free hand against her thigh. Pulling herself up from the comfortable sofa she put the cup down on the coffee table next to a bowl of potpourri and a coffee table book about the Yorkshire Dales.

"You hunt down the wifi code," she said, flicking through a pile of magazines on the table. "It'll probably be in a folder somewhere, porch way maybe. And I'll try and find some torches just in case we have a power cut and the missing family decide to give us a scare."

She gave Swift a sly grin and grabbed both their empty cups to wash up.

"You won't be smiling if the lights do go out, O'Malley," he said, swinging his legs around with a groan. "You'll be begging me to come and sleep in your room to protect you."

"Ha!" Annie blurted, hoping the lights don't go out because she's not a fan of the dark, especially in a place she doesn't know well. "In your dreams, Swift. In your dreams."

At home, Annie kept her matches and torches in the cupboard under the sink of the little kitchenette. Mainly because there's not a lot of storage space, but also that cupboard is the resting place of odds and sods that don't have a proper home. She pulled open the twinning cupboard of the cottage and felt a mild sense of annoyance at how Mrs Hinch it was. Nothing was out of place, even the bottles of bleach were all facing outwards in size order. Annie didn't realise it came in so many varieties. No sign of either a torch or matches though.

With one last pantry sized cupboard to try, Annie straightened up and pulled the handle. The door was heavier than the others, pulling not only the facade of the cupboard, but the surround away with it too. A cold, damp gust of air pushed through the gap and swirled around her ankles.

"Swift," Annie shouted, heaving the door as far open as she dared. "Come look at this."

The cupboard gave way to a small staircase leading down to the depths of the cottage. Dusty cobwebs curled around the corners, flapping about in the stale breeze.

"What have you unearthed, O'Malley?" Swift said, coming up behind her and peering over her shoulder. "This is supposed to be a getaway. Don't turn it into a busman's holiday, please."

Hanging from a small hook on the back of the cellar door was a small torch that looked much like Swift's police issued one.

"Ah ha." Annie grabbed it, ignoring Swift, and clicked it on. The beam was powerful enough to bounce around the stairwell.

Steps, worn in the middle from decades of use, led down into the gloom. Annie took them carefully, swiping the beam of light back and forth to light the way. She could feel and hear Swift behind her, never one to miss out on an adventure.

The stairs swung to the left and back on themselves, Annie held a hand up to pass under what must be the floor of the kitchen, careful not to knock her head against the concrete. They opened to a small cellar room, probably the size of the footprint of the cottage. It smelt damp and musty, but it didn't feel unused. More that the smell was emanating from a leak or an old wet swimsuit left in the washing machine. Anne could sense that the cellar wasn't empty before she saw what it had to offer.

"What on earth," Swift whistled through his teeth. "Trust you to end up staying not only somewhere that is haunted by a missing family, but also still full of what looks like their belongings."

The beam of torchlight stopped on a pile by the far wall. There were suitcases, baby toys, a crib, pictures in frames standing on small old pieces of chintzy furniture. Dusty, floral curtains draped over an armchair in the shape of a shell. A leather pouffe was pushed right into the corner of the room, and sitting on top of it, as though waiting for its owner to return and play, was a Cabbage Patch doll, arms held out towards Annie, a hopeful look etched on its round face.

FOUR

"THIS ISN'T AT ALL CREEPY," ANNIE SAID sarcastically, stepping up to the doll.

"Don't touch it!" Swift shouted, grabbing Annie's arm before she could pick it up. "They might not like that."

He edged away, his voice faltering as though he'd just remembered he didn't believe in ghosts.

"They?" Annie asked, dropping her arm, and stepping away from the belongings.

Swift ran a hand through his hair.

"Yeah, you know, them. The ghosts? Wooo." he wiggled his fingers around in front of his face.

"You just told me you don't believe in ghosts." Annie couldn't take her eyes off the limp curtains draped over the chair. "Besides, aren't you even a little bit curious? I mean, look at all this stuff."

She picked up a photograph, blurry behind a layer of thick dust. The metal frame was speckled green with age and damp. Using her sleeve, Annie wiped away the dust to reveal a happy looking couple with a young baby. The man was tall, dark, with a bushy beard and bell bottom cords. The woman was slight, her paisley dress mostly covered by a hand wrapped baby carrier. He had his arm casually slung around her shoulders, and they both beamed into the camera, Crow Cottage behind them and an old Ford in the drive.

"Look," Annie held the picture out for Swift to see. Hunched over because of the low ceiling, he moved towards her and took it from her hands. "Do you think this is them?"

He studied the photograph, brow rumpled. "Most probably." He nodded, handing it back. "Who did you rent this place from? Do you think it's their extended family?"

"I don't know," Annie said, putting the photo back down and angling it so it faced the stairs. There was a newspaper article next to the photo, the same picture in black and white with the words MISSING printed above, she folded it up and pocketed it to read later. "But after all this time, why keep all this stuff down here? Do you think they're hoping the family will come back?"

"It's a bit weird if you ask me," Swift said, shuddering rather dramatically. "I mean, photos and mementoes I get, but… curtains? Surely, even if they did come back now, they're not going to want to keep *those*."

The torch in Annie's hand flickered and plunged them momentarily into darkness, shadows pooling in the corners. It grew colder too, as though the cellar was an old icehouse. Annie shook the torch, not entirely sure that it would bring back the light, but that's what people in the movies did. It worked, but the light was fading and the darkness in the corners of the room was encroaching on them. Swift hesitated by Annie's side, but she could feel the tension in his body filling the small chamber with static. Without thinking too hard about it, Annie gathered up a folder bursting with papers and the soft doll and turned to leave, Swift close on her heels.

Back up in the warmth of the cottage, Annie felt a bit silly about how she'd reacted. But there was still something making her feel uncomfortable and she couldn't figure out what it was. Swift appeared in the doorway, edging out of the cellar like a contortionist. He pushed the cupboard door shut behind him and went straight to the fridge.

"Want one?" he asked, pulling out a beer.

Annie shook her head and flicked the switch back on the kettle. For reasons she didn't know yet, she needed her wits about her. There was a tap on her elbow as she stared at her reflection in the dark window, waiting for the kettle. Swift stood next to her, gesturing at the doll she gripped tightly in her hand and the folder tucked under her arm.

"Any reason you picked those two to release from their tomb?" he asked. "I feel like you might have unleashed some sort of curse by bringing that thing up here."

He was pointing to the Cabbage Patch doll with its black eyes sewn too close together. It felt damp to touch, sticky almost, and far too cold, as though the cellar was still clinging to it.

"Thought I'd get a better look at them up here, that's all," Annie replied, mostly about the folder that was starting to dig into her side. "Grab this would you?"

Swift's mouth pulled into a grimace before he realised she was talking about the paperwork. He took it from under her arm and disappeared off to the living room. Annie held the doll up and studied its face. It hadn't felt right leaving it down in the cellar, but now it was up here amongst the real-world Annie half wished she'd left it sitting on the pouffe where it had no doubt sat for the last thirty-odd years. Its orange hair was twisted in two amateur plaits, tied at the end with a clashing pink ribbon. The dress was grubby with use, the way children's toys all turn a shade of grey with the amount of love bestowed upon them. Somebody had cared a great deal about this Cabbage Patch doll,

41

so Annie sat her on the windowsill of the kitchen and made herself a strong coffee.

"Listen to this," Swift said to Annie as she carried her coffee and a couple of packs of biscuits from the welcome hamper to the living room. She chucked a pack in his direction and took her seat back on the sofa under the stairs. Swift cleared his throat and read from a sheet of paper in his hands. *"To the Harper family, we are looking forward to welcoming you to Butlins this summer, where your holiday dreams will come true."*

Annie scoffed, though she'd have leapt at the chance to holiday in Butlins as a child. As it was, Annie's mum thought holidays were best spent at home with family, and then when half her family disappeared holidays weren't even an afterthought.

"Is it just a load of crap?" she asked about the folder of paperwork spilling out onto the sofa next to Swift.

"It's certainly a few years' worth of mundane bills and letters, that's for sure," Swift replied, edging forward on the sofa. "But this letter was dated in April of eighty-four."

Annie felt her whole-body itch, her scalp crawled with invisible insects. "But didn't they go missing in May?"

Swift nodded, understanding.

"Why book a holiday when you know you're about to leave?"

He shrugged at Annie's question. "Exactly."

"Hmmm."

"Hmm, indeed."

They looked at each other over the small living room, the idea that this family didn't just up and leave was leaching into Annie's skin like the damp in the cellar. She gripped her coffee cup tighter to try and heat up her hands.

"I wonder if..." Annie started, staring at the liquid in her cup, her mind working nineteen to the dozen.

Swift held up his hand to stop her. "Before you say it, and I know exactly what you're going to say, remember why you're here."

Annie opened her mouth and then closed it again. Swift really did know her better than she knew herself sometimes.

"But they might have family who are wondering what happened to them?" she said, unable to dampen her curiosity. "Just like I'm searching for Mim, they might be out there searching for the Harpers."

"While their stuff is left in the cellar of their old house, rented out for money?" Swift replied, his top teeth gripping his bottom lip so tightly it turned white. "It makes no sense."

"Exactly," Annie said. "Nothing about this makes any sense. And I can't help but wonder why. Don't tell me you're not in the least bit curious? That your police radar isn't going off in that beautiful skull of yours with a million and one questions."

Swift put down the holiday booking on top of the card folder where it slid onto the sofa. He stood and walked to the window, scanning the front garden with his hand held to the glass to shield the light from the room. In the reflection Annie caught a glimpse of his face, relaxed and happy and probably well in need of a holiday that didn't involve digging into the disappearance of a local family. He swore quietly and turned back to the room, perching on the sill.

"I found the wifi code when you were playing Indiana Jones through there," he said, crossing one ankle over the other. "A quick search showed me that there was a huge police hunt for family; husband, wife, and a baby boy, but it threw up nothing and the case is still cold. Get this though, I had to scroll through *loads* of links to the haunted house and the famous village before I found anything about the actual disappearance. It's like a landmark that people visit, a crappy Stonehenge. No offence to the cottage because it's actually quite sweet, if a bit cramped."

"Cramped?" Annie raised an eyebrow. "This cottage is about three times the size of my home."

"You know what I mean," Swift waved a hand. "Anyway, that wasn't my point. What with you and that creepy doll, and the pile of belongings in the cellar, and that holiday form, I can't help being curious too."

An owl hooted somewhere nearby, a haunting sound that was perfectly fitting for the cottage. Past Swift's head at the window, Annie could just about make out the movement of bats in the night sky. If it wasn't for the fact she was dressed in her comfiest loungewear and hadn't brushed her hair at all today, Annie thought that she and Swift could be in a horror movie.

"So?" she asked, drawing out the word like a question. "Can we have a little look into the disappearance? While we're here? It might open doors to ask people about Mim, too."

Swift lifted the can of beer to his mouth and drained the last of it. Running his fingers over his lips he rolled his eyes in Annie's direction.

"Okay," he acquiesced, as though he wasn't gunning at the bit to investigate too. "In fact, why don't we take a walk into the village, buy some supper, and see if we can get some more info from the locals while we're there?"

Annie jumped up from her seat and drained her coffee. She grabbed her coat and bag from where she'd dropped them at the foot of the stairs and was slipping her feet into her shoes before he could change his mind. Swift grabbed his wallet from the coffee table and passed Annie at the porch way, pulling the door open to the cool night. The smell of log fires sat heavily in the air, rich and pungent, it reminded Annie of bonfire night. She switched the lights off behind them and pocketed the keys to the cottage, following Swift out onto the weeds. He unlocked the car and ducked into the driver's seat. Annie was about to suggest that they walk when he reappeared with a Maglite torch and a smile.

"Shall we?" he asked, holding out his elbow for Annie.

"Let's," she agreed, taking his arm and following the beam of light designed for night-time crime scenes that shone their way down to the tarmac lane.

"Oh, and O'Malley?" He turned to Annie with a grin. "Thanks for saying my skull is beautiful."

Annie flushed scarlet and focused on the road under her feet, glad of the cover of darkness.

"What do you think happened to the Harpers?" Swift asked, as they passed by the entrance to the church. "Do you think there's a killer out there who's gotten away with murder these last forty-odd years?"

Annie scanned the graveyard, the tombstones sticking out of the ground like wonky teeth.

"I don't know," she said. "But something is telling me that if there is a killer out there, even after all this time, they won't have gone too far."

FIVE

THE UNLIT BONFIRE ROSE OUT OF THE NIGHT SKY LIKE a giant spider. Beyond it, on the green, groups of people were still milling around. Their own smaller, disposable BBQs made the air around it wobble, as though the tall criss-crossed stack of logs were on acid.

Or maybe I'm the one on acid, Annie thought as she dropped Swift's arm and stepped over the small railing onto the grass.

Wildflowers grew around the edge of the duckpond, a scattering of cornflower blues dotted with colourful tulips and subdued cow parsley that made up for lack of colour with its towering height. The ducks were huddled together on the bank, their heads tucked into their wings, perhaps to stave off the noise of the families gathered on the green.

Annie pulled her coat around her body, hugging it against herself as she walked with Swift towards the nuclear groups. Their communal chatter was upbeat, dotted with laughter and the fizz pop of cans being cracked open. The little shop they'd visited earlier was closed up for the night, the lights switched off and the person who'd served them was sitting on the grass in the middle of the green with a couple of teenage boys and a small terrier. The pub next door to the shop was glowing with life through its criss-crossed leaded windows. The smell of fried food permeated the air and Annie felt her stomach shift over, unsatisfied with the small pack of biscuits she'd eaten earlier.

Another group of children played catch in the dim evening light, throwing a worn tennis ball over the heads of three tired looking adults. A couple lay on the grass, one propped up between the other's legs, sharing a flask of something giving off steam. Annie counted maybe fifteen or twenty people congregating on the green.

"They're all very friendly, aren't they? "Annie whispered. "Apart from Pizza Pete downstairs, I have no idea who my neighbours are. And these guys are all out here on a Monday night as though it's a Sunday lunchtime in the middle of summer!"

"Just because you're anti-social, doesn't mean this is weird," Swift whispered back, stopping and perusing the groups.

"I didn't say weird," Annie corrected him. "I said friendly. And you're worse than I am, I bet you couldn't name even *one* of *your* neighbours."

Swift popped the collar on his jacket and started up towards the people.

"What are you doing?" Annie hissed at him, standing her ground. "We can't just invade someone's dinner picnic!"

"Why not?" Swift replied, heading towards a group of middle-aged women with a bottle of Cava. "Let's pick a willing group of suspects though."

Annie laughed at Swift's confidence and skipped to catch up with him. The group of women turned at their approach, a few of them giving Swift the up and down look of approval that came with the territory. Annie guessed that Swift had picked them on purpose now she could see their welcome committee. They all had a glossy-red cheeked look about them, resulting probably from the three empty bottles strewn beside their make-shift fire-pit. They shuffled around on their tweed blankets to get a better look at Annie and Swift. There were four of them, all about the same age as Annie's mum.

"Are you joining us?" one asked, her hand wrapped tightly around a plastic tumbler full of fizzy wine, her casual outfit looked like it was made entirely of cashmere and silk.

"If you're offering a sip of that, we are," Swift replied, as smooth as ever.

Annie watched in awe as the four women parted to make space on the blanket. She took a seat between Swift and one of the older women who smelt like a Jo Malone store. From the fizzy wine, the casual chic, the expensive shoes, and the subtle designer accessories shared out equally between the four women, Annie guessed they were all on better salaries than both her and Swift. Probably put together.

She took a cup of Cava and thanked the woman who handed it to her, her red nails perfectly filed.

"Are you local?" another woman asked the pair, crossing her lithe legs under her like a yoga teacher.

"You're not then?" Swift answered. "What brings you to Ethlake?"

He raised his cup in a cheer and took a sip, sighing.

"We've come for the week to check out the hauntings," the woman at the edge of the group said. She'd been quiet up until then, but her answer was given with sparkling eyes. "We wanted to stay at Crow Cottage but it was already booked out, so we're at a Travelodge about ten miles away. Bit of a nuisance as we'd had this planned for months, but apparently Crow Cottage gets booked out years in advance."

Annie opened her mouth to say she'd only booked it last month, but the eager looks on the women's faces made her falter and shut it again.

"Why here?" Swift asked, innocently.

The women exchanged a conspiratorial look between them and the one who'd invited them over to join them spoke.

"There's a rumour," she said leaning in towards Swift. Annie saw the way her skin shone in the firelight, smooth and taut.

"What kind of rumour?" Swift asked, mirroring her lean.

"That there's a witch who lives in the woods around the village." The woman's voice was so quiet that Annie had to lean in too, just to catch the odd word. "It's rumoured that she sacrifices children to make the village prosper. She appears every so often and takes what's not hers to blood-let to the gods."

Annie sighed, ripples of unease contracting her lungs. What if Mim had gotten mixed up in this while she was staying in Ethlake? What if the talk of disappearances and witches and sacrificed children had opened up old wounds in her sister? Was that why she wasn't here anymore?

"We're going to find her cottage tomorrow," Jo Malone said in a hushed voice. "It's abandoned, but we've got a way of contacting the Witch, haven't we, Jessica?"

The alpha female of the pack, Jessica, gave a wry smile.

"We're what you'd call, modern day witches." The air twisted around Annie, stroking at her throat with cold fingers.

The fire crackled between them all, sparks jumping up into the night sky. Over by the woods at the far end of the village green a flock of birds soared into the sky with a clatter of wings and branches. Something had spooked them. Annie shifted uncomfortably on the blanket. All four women were staring at her, their glassy eyes flickering with the reds and yellows of the fire, shadows dancing across their stretched skin. They were one too many to be The Wayward Sisters of Macbeth, and far too glamorous, but Annie felt like they were brewing trouble all the same.

"I thought modern day witches were only for good magic, Wiccans aren't you?" Annie spluttered scratching at her neck.

Jessica sat upright and clapped her hands together, breaking whatever tension had been twisted tight by their story. The four of them broke away in laughter, the noise made Annie squirm.

"We're only pulling your leg," Jessica said, when she'd caught her breath. Her mascara had clumped in the outside corner of her eye, sticking her lashes together when she blinked. "Zoe here is about to wed her third husband so we're escaping for a few days, and we wanted to do something different. Ghost hunting seemed like a hoot. It's a set itinerary and we will be off to the witch's hut tomorrow but there'll be no summoning the dead. Just a load of fifty-year-olds taking selfies with their friends."

"Well you certainly had me going," Swift laughed, tapping Jessica's knee gently with his palm. "I hope you girls have a great holiday and…"

"Wait," Annie interrupted him, addressing Jessica. "The rumours about the witch stealing children, was that bit true?"

"Oh yes," the woman replied, the group growing quiet around her once again. "Very much so. Crow Cottage missing family? Their baby was the youngest member of the village when they went missing. It's said the witch took the baby to sacrifice for the sake of the village, and the parents were collateral damage."

"Oh god!" Annie said, thinking about the Cabbage Patch doll she'd rescued from the cellar.

"A young baby, only a few months," red talons answered. Annie breathed out a slow, controlled breath, catching Swift's eye. He gave her the smallest shake of his head and she knew not to push it.

"But the weirdest thing is," Jessica said, and there was no humour in her face now. "It's only a little girl who is said to haunt the cottage. No members of the family have ever been seen. What does that tell you about the disappearance, hey? If the little girl is the only ghost?"

SIX

ANNIE AND SWIFT SAID THEIR GOODBYES TO THE women and thanked them for the Cava. It had left a sickly taste on Annie's tongue and a sense of unease in her stomach. She didn't want to talk to any of the other people sitting out on the green. The idea to look into the missing family was already taking over her thoughts and this break was supposed to be for her sister. Swift had been right to question her motives, because she was already regretting them.

"You look like you're getting hungry," Swift said, looking at her like he might do a wild, big cat. "Shall we check out the pub food? It smells fried and bad for me and that's how I like it."

His joke worked, Annie smiled and remembered that they were away on a holiday, and she could eat pub food and drink a cart load of gin and all would be well.

If Ethlake itself was like something out of a Miss Marple set, then The Stag was just as clichéd. It offered low slung ceilings striped with beams, a wonky wooden floor, and a roaring fireplace with horseshoes nailed on the mantel. It was only half full, an old man and woman sat around a small table, spooning curry onto naan bread, and a family of four gathered around on a couple of sofas with a pack of cards and the most delicious looking mezze between them.

The barman had a tea-towel slung over his shoulder and a welcome smile on his face. He must have been about Annie's age, with rosy, red cheeks and a chin full of stubble. His t-shirt stretched over his stomach and hinted at a love of beer.

"What can I get you two?" he asked them as Annie took one of the bar stools tucked away around the far end of the bar and Swift sat next to her.

"Gin please," Annie said a little too quickly.

The barman laughed. "Any tonic with that or are you just out to get pissed?"

"Just a splash," Annie smiled back. "If I have to?"

Swift ordered a beer for himself and paid the barman, grabbing a couple of menus from a stack on the bar and handing one to Annie. It looked like proper pub food, all the carbs and not much else. It was perfect. Annie ordered fish and chips and mushy peas and

Swift went for the steak and kidney pudding with mash and gravy. A couple of minutes later and a tall glass landed in front of Annie, condensation dripping down the side and a refreshing fizz misting over the top. She took a sip, savouring the coolness and enjoying the way it shrivelled up her lips with the strength of the alcohol the barman had added.

"That's good," she said, lifting her glass in a cheers. "Thank you."

"Welcome," the barman replied, eyeing Swift out of the corner of his eyes. "I can tell a girl in need of a drink when I see one."

Annie slumped on her stool, resting her chin on her palms and her elbows on the sticky bar top. She carried on drinking through her straw, happy not to have to lift her head.

"Is it that obvious?" she said through the straw stuck between her lips.

"Well, you're not here on holiday, are you?" the barman added, sucking his teeth. "I can tell that much. And even the longest drive wouldn't have people looking quite as weary as you two. No offence."

Annie glanced at Swift, in need of his support. His soft smile and tired eyes buoyed her as she knew they would. The barman, more than most, would have answers about Mim, Annie just knew it. He busied himself drying glasses from the dishwasher and stacking them on a rubber mat above the optics.

"It's a holiday of sorts." Annie pushed herself upright and retied her hair in a top knot. At least her bun could pull her face upwards like the proverbial Essex facelift. "I'm actually searching for my little sister."

"Your little sister, hey?" he mirrored, still stacking glasses. "Are you guys from around here? I don't recognise you and…"

He hesitated and glanced again at Swift. If Annie didn't know any better, she could have sworn he'd been about to say 'and I'd definitely recognise someone who looked like you'. That age old chat up line she hadn't heard since her clubbing days. The barman was attractive in a homely way, but Annie had sworn off men since her last boyfriend had tried to inject her with bubonic plague. Besides, she was only here for a week and Crow Cottage was too small for a casual hook up.

"I was told she'd been here recently," Annie interrupted, putting the man out of his misery. An angry red flush ran across his throat like someone had taken a knife to it. "Did you meet her? Her name is Mim, she's twenty-one. She was definitely here about a year ago, and from what I've heard so far, not here anymore."

Annie searched the barman's face for clues he recognised Mim. It wasn't much to go on, she knew this, just an age and a name that she might not even be using anymore. But she had to start somewhere. The barman stacked the last glass and threw the tea towel back over his shoulder, shaking his head.

"Don't think I recognise a Mim, no," he said, and Annie's heart sank back to her empty stomach. "But we are the village of disappearing families so you're in the right place."

He leant over the bar, the earlier embarrassment long gone, replaced with a twinkle in his blood-shot eyes.

"Have you heard about the Harpers?" he said, conspiratorially. "They vanished into thin air just over forty years ago now, no trace of any of them. Rumour has it…"

"They were taken by the witch and their ghosts still haunt the cottage, yes, yes," Swift interrupted impatiently. "Could you do me a favour and go and check on our food, please?"

The barman looked as though Swift had just slapped the words from his mouth. He pushed away from the bar with a concerned look at Annie and disappeared into the kitchen.

"Swift?" Annie said, batting him on the shoulder.

"Oh god, really?" he replied. "You want to listen to that old story again? It's as though they have a linear mindset when it comes to Ethlake. Mim probably left because she was bored out of her skull listening to these fools go on about the bloody ghost."

"But what if he knows something about my sister?" Annie asked angrily. "And now he won't tell me because you were so rude."

"He wouldn't have told you with me here anyway," Swift shrugged. "He thinks I'm your boyfriend."

"God forbid," Annie whispered under her breath.

"I heard that," Swift said.

"You were supposed to," she replied.

They fell into a silence, sipping their drinks and letting the songs from the tinny radio pass between them.

"You don't think it's weird?" Swift said, as the Carpenters crooned about *just beginning*.

Annie slurped the last of her gin, feeling her head lighten.

"What's weird?" she asked, wondering if two would be too many.

Swift drained his own beer and put down his glass. He checked across the bar at the old couple and the family. Annie recognised the look in his eye, he was like a dog with a bone.

"So far you've asked the two most likely people in the village to have met your sister," he said, quietly. "And they've both denied it."

Weird? No. It was more of a sadness that she felt. If the local shop and pub didn't know anything about Mim then maybe she had never been here at all.

"Maybe Harry lied," she said, sadly, remembering the way the doctor had garbled the name of the village on his deathbed, boasted about knowing where Mim was.

"Why?" Swift threw his hands out. "What reason would he have for lying to you? For starters, he thought *you* were going to die, he could have told you his PIN number and given you his card. Or told you his deepest darkest secret. There would have been no reason to lie to you about something he didn't realise was so significant in your life. Then when he did know how important it was to you, he was already dying, it was just a way to rub it in, to have one last piece of information over you. It was about control."

Annie knew this, she also knew that when Harry was garbling his last breath, he wasn't lying. She could tell from his face, through the evilness had been someone who wanted her to know he was better than she was. And it had worked. All those years Annie had spent looking for Mim, the private detectives, the money spent, and nothing. And a doctor had managed to track her down with what had sounded like no trouble at all.

"Then what?" she snapped. "You think the whole village is lying instead?"

Swift raised his eyebrows and hushed her, drawing his lips together in a silent *shh*.

"Oh," she whispered. "You do think they're lying?"

A rattle of cutlery made Annie startle, and the barman laid a knife and fork on a napkin in front of each of Annie and Swift. He gave her a short smile, but it was in act only, his eyes looked as cold as the ice melting in her empty glass. He went back through the curtain to the kitchen and Annie spun on her stool to face Swift.

"But why would they lie to me about Mim?" she whispered, frantically. "Do you think something has happened to her? Do you think she was taken by the witch?"

A huge platter of fish and chips was laid in front of Annie, the fish so large it didn't fit on the plate. The chips hung on to the side precariously, and a splodge of mushy peas with a dash of mint sauce drizzled in the middle finished the plate. It drew Annie's attention as her stomach turned over itself with hunger. Swift thanked the barman for his pie and mash, his gravy rather ungenerously didn't even cover the pastry.

"We'll talk about this later," he said, pointedly to Annie. "And I'll shoot off a quick message to Tink and Page to get them to look into *things*."

Annie nodded slowly, understanding, as the barman went back to his tea towel and glasses. DS Belle Lock, otherwise known as Tink, and DC Tom Page made up the rest of the Major Crime Unit, or MCU, at their station. They were both back in Norfolk, working on a drugs bust, while their DI accompanied Annie on a wild goose chase.

Annie unwrapped her knife and fork from the red napkin and started eating. It was delicious, and she soon became wrapped in a blanket of exhaustion from the travel and the cottage and the weird village. It took all her effort to finish up her fish and chips and stay upright on her stool.

"You look as beat as I feel," Swift said, putting down his cutlery, his plate still half full. "Let's get back to the cottage."

The barman looked over from where he had been chopping lemons, knife poised mid-air.

"*You're* the couple staying at Crow Cottage?" he asked, forehead pinched.

Annie nodded, dropping down from the seat.

"We're here for the week." She slipped her coat on and fished out her purse.

"Put that away," the barman said, wiping his hands on the same tea towel he'd dried the glasses with. "Your first meal is on the house. Courtesy of the Harper ghosts. I didn't realise you two were hunters."

"We're…" Annie started to disagree with the barman. They weren't ghost hunters, she just wanted to find her sister. But Swift interrupted.

"Thank you," he held out his hand to the barman. "Sorry about earlier, I was hangry. I'm Joe, this is Annie. We're excited to be here for the May Day celebrations. We've heard so much about the village. It was just coincidence that Annie's sister stayed here a while back too. We'll be seeing more of you this week, I'm sure."

"Lewis," the barman said, shaking Swift's hand with a deliberate force. "And yes, the celebrations will start to ramp up this week. And there's the May Day party on the green on Sunday, I hope you'll both be here for that? If you survive the ghosts, that is."

Swift pulled on his coat and took Annie's arm, leading her out of the warm pub.

"What was that about?" she asked him as they walked back along the now deserted lane to the cottage. "Suddenly he's your new best friend. Why tell him we're ghost hunters?"

Swift's arm tensed under her hand, so briefly she would have missed it if she didn't know him so well.

"There is something not quite right about this place," he replied, clearing his throat. "If we let people think we're ghost hunters then at least they'll know how to treat us. I get the feeling they don't like strangers asking questions unless they're to do with the haunted cottage and the missing family."

"Why, though?"

"That, my dear O'Malley, we shall have to find out."

SEVEN

Tuesday

ANNIE AWOKE THE NEXT MORNING, RESTED, FRESH, and ready for their first full day in Ethlake. The smell of bacon had her sliding from the comfortable bed, and washing, and dressing in record time. Swift was standing in the kitchen, back to the door, busy at the hob with a frying pan when she made it down the stairs.

"I don't know about any ghosts," she said, grabbing the coffee pot from its holder and pouring herself a cup, she added a splash of creamy milk. "But I slept like the dead. How about you?"

The small table was set for breakfast; Annie took a seat and let Swift carry on pottering around the kitchen, just like last year when he'd been looking after her because of her broken ankle. He was a dab hand with anything domesticated and Annie knew not to interrupt his process.

"Hmm," Swift replied, cracking eggs into the pan. "The airing cupboard in my room is home to the noisiest boiler known to humankind. It felt like every hour, on the hour, it would kick into life just to warm the water in the tank in case someone wanted to shower in the middle of the night."

There were a brief few seconds where Annie wondered whether to offer to swap rooms, but it vanished pretty much as quickly as it arrived.

"Maybe we could get you some earplugs from the little shop today," she offered with a smile instead.

"It's fine," Swift replied as the toaster popped. He loaded toast, eggs, bacon, mushrooms, and tomatoes onto two plates and carried them over to the table, putting one in front of Annie. "Tuck in. It's only a few nights, besides it meant I got up early to email Tink and Page. I want them to investigate the missing family. There's a lot about this that is making me question what the police actually did back then, and I'd like them to have a quiet dig around."

"Totally out of our jurisdiction, isn't it?" Annie asked, savouring a runny egg and crispy bacon forkful.

"Yep." Swift shrugged. "That's why they're doing it quietly. And, I say we eat this then head back into the village to meet some more locals. We're here to get information on your sister and I want to see what it all feels like during the day. The sun is shining, and some fresh air might help me stay awake!"

Less than an hour later they were pulling on their shoes and heading out the front door of Crow Cottage. The air felt warm, breezeless, the way the weather sometimes hints at the pull of summer. Annie breathed in the scents around her, the smell of cut grass and farms floated in the air with the pollen. Round bellied bees buzzed across their driveway, bumping softly into the dandelions generously scattered along the gravel. A lonely sheep bleated in the distance. It was idyllic, Annie thought, enjoying the moment.

The church towered above them as they walked down the lane towards the village centre. With the sun behind them, both the bell tower and the water tower looked like charcoal silhouettes on a chalk drawing. The bell rang out, making Annie jump. Laughing at herself, she listened to the ten peels, as she followed Swift along the lane.

"Could you live somewhere like this?" he asked her as she caught up to him.

"I think the setting is idyllic," she said, plucking a long piece of grass from the verge and chewing the sweet end. "But I'm not sure I could be so isolated. You?"

"Yeah, same," Swift replied. "It's the isolation that would get me. But also, the community here seems very close knit. You wouldn't be able to go for a piss in the woods without everyone knowing about it before you'd even zipped up your flies."

"Do you often piss in the woods?" Annie laughed.

"God," Swift said, bypassing her question. "Imaging having an affair in this place. You'd be strung up on the bonfire. Probably both parties. Do you think that's what the pole is for?"

Swift motioned to the village green and the May Pole sitting pretty amongst the daisies.

"I'm going to assume that's a rhetorical question and you do know that young children will be dancing and singing around that come Sunday?" Annie watched the ducks floating calmly on the surface of the pond. Their bodies sending pools of ripples out in cascading rings.

"Having danced around a fair few in my youth, I can confirm your assumptions," Swift said, drawing his phone from his pocket as it started to ring. "And up until yesterday when we saw it, I had blocked the whole memory of dancing around a May Pole from my mind. What a flashback that was."

He shuddered then swiped to answer his phone. Annie left him to it, stepping over the low railings onto the village green. They were the only two out this morning, Annie guessed that most people would be at work or school. She cut across the grass to the pond, the ducks swimming a little quicker over to the far side of the water. Had Mim spent time on this village green? Given how much of a community spirit there was in Ethlake, Annie guessed that Mim would have spent a lot of time here, maybe throwing bread for the ducks or picking daisies to make a chain. Given how much Annie's dad enjoyed the countryside and had taken Mim to live in a commune, she wondered if her dad had ever been here too. Had he walked across the grass with her sister, thrown bread alongside her? She wondered if her dad had ever thought about her after all those years, or if his focus had been entirely on Mim, the rest of his family long forgotten.

A golden retriever burst through the trees that banked the edge of the green, its shaggy coat glossy in the sunshine. With its tongue lolling out of its almost smiling mouth, Annie watched as it leapt into the air and landed with a resounding splash in the pond. The ducks took flight, even the younger ones flapped hard and soared from the water, following their parents into the woods.

"Sandy!" A voice shouted from the woods. "Come back here right this instant, you naughty boy."

Sandy did no such thing, so happy doggy-paddling through the green water. The voice was followed shortly after by a man Annie recognised from the pub the previous night. His white hair was less glossy than Sandy's, and his short legs did nothing to help speed up his chase. When he reached the water's edge, the man bent double at the waist and put his hands on his knees to stop him nose diving the grass. His back rose and fell as he tried to catch his breath.

Not quite sure what to do, Annie watched as Sandy swam happily about the pond, his glossy coat slowly turning the same colour as the algae that bevelled the surface of the water. The man by her side stopped huffing like a steam engine and straightened, swigging water from a bottle of Evian to try and cool down. They both watched as the dog swam to the edge and hauled itself out of the water, its fur lagging like a wet flannel.

"Stupid bloody dog," the man said, with a lot of love in his voice. "It's a good job we love them, hey?"

He looked at Annie and smiled knowingly. Annie only had a pot plant to look after so she had no idea if she'd love a dog, but the way it jogged towards its owner, tail wagging sending sprays of water this way and that just like a farmer's irrigation system made her think she'd probably agree. Though perhaps a cat might be better suited for her tiny studio.

"He looked like he was having fun," Annie said in reply.

"I always put his lead back on before we get to the edge of the woods," the man said, shaking his head. "This has happened more than once. But Sandy was too quick for my old bones today. He ran off as I was unravelling it."

He held up a retractable lead in his hands and Annie laughed.

"I was too distracted by the ghost hunters," the man went on. "They're traipsing through the woods as we speak. Heading back from the *witch's hut* I imagine."

Annie detected a hint of irritation in the man.

"You'll have to send Sandy back into the woods, he looks a bit like a ghoul now," she said as the dog waddled over.

His coat was gloopy with green algae, only his head remained a golden yellow. The man laughed and clipped Sandy's lead to the collar.

"You know, that's not a bad idea." He held out his hand. "I'm Alfred Hankin, you can call me Alf, are you staying nearby?"

"Annie," she said, shaking Alf's hand. "Yes, we're up at Crow Cottage."

Alf's eyebrows shot up into his thatch of silver hair.

"You're staying at Crow Cottage and you're not on the ghost hunt?" He looked at her curiously, mistrusting. Swift's words from the previous night in the pub echoed in her head.

"Oh," she waved a hand in dismissal. "We slept in, you know how it is after a busy day and a long drive. And we're here all week, so I'm sure we'll have another chance to check out the tour."

Alf nodded slowly and over his shoulder Annie saw the four women from the picnic eagerly gathered around a young man as they exited the woods further up the green.

"Is that them?" Annie asked.

Alf turned his attention from Annie to the gaggle of ghost hunters.

"Yup," he said. "That's Gerry Needham, tour guide extraordinaire. He knows all there is to know about the Harpers and Crow Cottage. He'll sign you up if you want to book in for another day."

Gerry Needham was about Annie's age, maybe a little older. He was tall and stocky and dressed like a farmer. He looked over past the women surrounding him directly at Annie and Alf. Even from across the green, Annie could see his eyes narrow, his attractive face pinched. The women soon drew his attention back to them, but Annie couldn't help wonder why

Gerry seemed to be already annoyed with her yet they'd never even met.

"I'd best get Sandy here home and b-a-t-h-e-d," Alf said, spelling out the word as if the dog could speak English.

He retracted Sandy's collar and the dog trotted back to his side.

"Before you go," Annie blurted, unable to help herself. "I'm also here to look for my sister, while I ghost hunt," she added making sure to keep the conversation light. "Do you know anyone called Mim? She'd look a bit like me, but early twenties. Stayed here a while back."

Alf looked up to the clouds dotted in the blue sky, he pursed his lips and paused before shaking his head.

"Nope," he said. "Though I do spend most of my time with the vicar, helping out in the church, so I'm not normally meeting new people. Must be off."

He didn't wait for a reply before he started walking back across the green. Sandy stayed still for a moment longer than his owner before bracing his legs and shaking his shaggy coat. A shower of slimy, green water shot from Sandy and sprayed Annie head to toe. The dog, now a little less green, ran off to catch up with Alf. The smell of the water dripping down Annie's face reminded her of the time she tried to make pancakes with eggs long past their sell by date.

Her little office-cum-flat had smelt like sewage for a week.

Swift came running over, biting down on his top lip, but the twinkle in his eye gave away how funny he was finding it.

"That was Tink on the phone," he said, grimacing as he got closer to the smell. "Do you want to go and shower, and I'll fill you in when you get back? I'll meet you in the pub for some lunch."

"Can you try to find out some info on Gerry Needham the tour guide, maybe book us on a ghost hunt," Annie replied, shaking her hands out.

"Will do, will do," Swift said, backing away a little. "But when you hear what Tink has dug up, the ghosts will be the last of your worries."

EIGHT

THE COTTAGE FELT COOL AS ANNIE SHUT THE DOOR behind her and stripped on the doorstep, turning the key in the lock, so no-one had to witness her running naked to the shower. She turned the dial to the hottest setting to warm the room up before she got in. Steam soon billowed around the small en-suite, misting the mirror and the window and fogging up Annie's vision. She wiped the mirror with her hand, just enough to see her green eyes staring back at her. Copper ringlets, damp with pond water stuck to her cheeks, like Ophelia if she'd made it out of the river before tragedy struck.

Grabbing a couple of clean towels from where she'd thrown them from her bed, Annie looked about for her wash bag to no avail. Sure she'd left it on the bedside table, Annie ducked her head under the bed to check it hadn't fallen in the night. Maybe she'd moved it earlier that morning? She scanned the room, but it was nowhere to be seen. Swift must have borrowed it. Annie chuckled at the thought of Swift using her moisturiser and darted back through to the en-suite, the cold now making her shiver. She turned the thermostat down to a temperature that wouldn't scold the skin off her bones and climbed under the hot water, using the tiny bottles of toiletries that had been left by the owner instead.

She washed quickly, unease settling in her bones. Talks of ghosts and curses and witches swirling around her thoughts now she was in the cottage alone. A patter of goosebumps lifted across Annie's arms and tickled their way up to her neck. She shook them out, trying to focus on the sun shining in through the misted window and the memory of Sandy jumping feet first into the pond. But the steam on the other side of the shower curtain moved about the room like bodies walking to and fro. With a drop in her stomach, Annie felt as though she wasn't the only one in the cottage. Her scalp crawled and her nose started to tickle. Slowly, she reached forwards, pinching the edge of the shower curtain between thumb and forefinger, her lungs burned as she held her breath. She whipped it back, ready to confront whoever was in the bathroom with her. But it was empty of all except the swirling mist.

"For god's sake, O'Malley," she said, her toes curling with the sound of her voice in the quiet. "Pull yourself together."

She pulled the curtain shut and grabbed the tiny bottle of shampoo, wanting to wash and get out of the cottage as quickly as possible. As the shampoo frothed in her curls, dripping down her forehead and stinging her eyes, Annie felt a cool draft whip around her ankles. It was as though someone had lifted the shower curtain and peeked in from below. She flung her eyes open, her vision blurred by the soap then the stabbing pain. Squeezing them closed again, Annie hurriedly rinsed the shampoo and turned off the water. Hurriedly stepping from the shower, Annie towel dried her hair as best as it would and palmed a handful of conditioner on her curls. There was no way she was getting back under the water to rinse it out, so she'd just have to make do with lank hair for the rest of the day.

The bedroom was awash with light from the window. Annie tucked her towel around her body and went to shut the curtains, plunging the bedroom into almost darkness with the blackout fabric. Blinking the sun from her eyes, Annie felt around for the light switch on the wall near the door. She knew it was there some-where, she just couldn't quite find it. Thoughts of brushing her fingers over the face of a ghostly child made a small whimper pop from between her lips. She bit down on them and almost whooped with joy to feel the plastic coating of the switch under her hands. Quickly flicking it on, Annie dropped onto the bed, exhausted with the adrenaline coursing through her veins. Looking about for her hairbrush to make sure the conditioner was at least covering all of her hair, Annie spotted her wash bag sitting innocuously on the top of the small dressing table. Her face crumpled with disbelief. She was sure she'd looked everywhere. Whistling out a tune between her teeth, Annie felt for her hairbrush on the bedside table, knowing it was there because putting it there was almost as instinctive to Annie as breathing.

It was gone. Not quite able to comprehend, Annie ducked her head to the gap between the bed and the table, sure she would see it stuck there by the side of the mattress. But there was nothing there except her pillow. She whispered a few choice swear words and ran her fingers through her hair instead, feeling the slick conditioner gather under her nails and knowing that she wouldn't be heading back in the bathroom to scrub it out.

Picking out a pair of jeans and a sweatshirt, Annie dragged them over her still damp skin. If she could just make it out of the cottage, Annie knew she'd be okay. Forgoing socks, she slipped the door open and started across the small landing to the stairs. The floorboards under her feet shifted, as though someone was standing on the other end of them. Glancing at Swift's bedroom door, Annie's blood ran cold.

A creak.

A clatter of metal on metal.

A whirring sound.

Annie didn't wait to see who was there. She bolted to the stairs, grabbing at the banister, she threw herself around and practically slid down to the hallway. Not looking back. Not wanting to see who was there. Her trainers were soaking, so Annie pushed her toes into her flip flops and tried to unlock the door. The whooshing noise above her head grew louder. Annie couldn't get purchase on the key, the conditioner coating her fingers making them slip and slide over the metal.

'Come on," she cried. "Come on."

But it was no good, every time she thought she had it gripped tightly enough, her fingers would lose purchase and bash painfully into the wood of the door. Swinging her head around, Annie saw the socks she'd pulled off earlier, grabbed at one and wrapped it around the key. A door creaked open at the top of the landing and the floorboards above her head shifted and shunted. Annie whimpered, feeling the key catch hold of the lock and turned it as quickly as she could. The warm air hit her face as she pulled the door towards her. Clutching the key still in the sock, Annie ran out, dragged the door closed and locked it in one slick movement.

A bluetit warbled on a branch above her head. It's song a calming tonic as Annie walked as fast as her flip flops would let her across the driveway and down the lane to the pub. Not once did she check behind her, for fear of seeing a face at the window.

"Annie," Swift called from the bar. "Perfect timing. What can I get you?" He clocked the wet hair and odd footwear. "Actually, I've got a table in the courtyard outside, go and sit down and I'll order you something."

Annie nodded and headed through the empty pub to a small corridor with the toilets and the back door. The courtyard was cobbled and enclosed by a small iron railing, not unlike the one circling the village green. It offered a scattering of wooden picnic benches with views of the larger farmhouses beyond the small cottages. Annie spotted where Swift had been sitting, his coat draped across a bench, but she opted for the table nearest the back where the sun was shining over the building. Her toes were already turning to ice, and she needed a little warmth.

"Here," Swift said, putting down a steaming cup of coffee in front of her. "I've ordered us some loaded chips too. Had to pay for this lot though, ghost hunters only get the one meal free."

Swift laughed and went to get his coat. Annie shivered just thinking about hunting ghosts.

"What's gotten into you?" he asked, draping his coat over the bench opposite Annie and sitting down.

"Oh, you know," she said, trying to shake herself out of it. "Just getting used to…"

She stopped, the look on Swift's face held no prisoners.

"Okay," she said, holding her hands up. "I'm sure there was someone in the cottage with me just now. I got scared, that's all."

'What," Swift said, leaning forwards over the table. "Like a ghost you mean?"

When it was spoken aloud, Annie couldn't help but feel stupid. But it had seemed so real back at the cottage.

"Maybe," she nodded. "I don't know. I thought there was someone in the shower with me. And then some of my stuff had been moved."

Annie remembered the steam, the way her wash bag had turned up.

'I don't know," she added, calm now Swift was with her. "Maybe I was imagining it. Did you borrow my hairbrush?"

A pink flush swept up Swift's cheeks.

"God, sorry," he said, cringing into his collar. "I meant to put it back. I forgot mine, and this mop is untameable by hand."

Annie breathed out a sigh of relief.

"Must have just been my overactive imagination," she said, circling her head on her neck to try and stretch out the tension. 'What did you want to tell me about Tink?"

Swift looked around his head twisting over one shoulder then the other.

"So," he said, placing both hands palms down on the rough wooden tabletop. "Tink and Page looked into the disappearance of the Harper family back in the eighties."

Annie nodded, sipping her coffee, her extremities slowly warming. Swift crossed his arms and leant forward on them.

"They could only access general info from the central database without setting warning bells off, but from what they said, there wasn't much to glean other than that anyway. From eyewitness accounts, the family were settled in Ethlake, the parents worked locally, the baby was loved and much wanted. Crime was low, very low, and on the occasion the local force was called in, it was for petty theft, small neighbour disputes, the odd stolen car, that kind of thing. No murder, gbh, abh, assaults, nothing."

"Okay," Annie said, pinching the bridge of her nose, she had a headache forming.

"So the police put their disappearance down to the family wanting a fresh start somewhere new," Swift added with a flourish.

"What?" Annie sat back upright. "That makes no sense. Happy families don't just disappear. What about friends? What about extended family?"

"That's what I said. But there was no extended family, except an elderly uncle of the father who lived out in Canada, long dead now. And their friends were all local."

"And did they think they'd run away too?" Annie couldn't get her head around it.

"Nope, but get this." Swift swept the courtyard for listening ears again. "Lots of families were leaving Ethlake at the time, the mines were closing, and they had no form of income. The police figured the Harpers were part of that exodus, even though they weren't miners. And not long after the family went missing, there was a sickness that swept the village. The locals stopped talking, and the ones who did only talked to the gutter press. Rumours of the witch started to circulate. That she took her sacrifice and made the village sick because the Harpers weren't enough to satiate her."

"Bloody heck," Annie whistled. "What idiots were spouting these rumours?"

"Our friendly barman, Lewis, and his pal Isla Hankinson, proprietor of the local shop."

NINE

"Let me get this straight," Annie said, stirring a sugar cube into her coffee, watching it bob around near the top, soaking up the liquid until it was too heavy to float. Her head was feeling just as heavy now the adrenaline was wearing off. "They were friends with the Harpers and let their disappearance be fobbed off as a sacrificial offering to an old woman who lived in the woods. No, wait, not just fobbed off, they actively encouraged people to think that?"

Swift's eyes widened and he discretely mouthed *shhh* at her. Footsteps behind her got louder and Lewis appeared over her shoulder with a large plate of melted cheese and bacon bits hiding a mound of chips. He put it on the table between Annie and Swift, giving them both cutlery and a casket of condiments. Annie felt her stomach rumble, though it didn't feel that long past Swift's fry-up. Glancing at her watch she was surprised to see it was almost two.

Lewis hovered around the table, gathering up Swift's empty glass and peering over the rim of Annie's coffee cup.

"When you've finished your lunch, I don't suppose you'd like to see something exciting, would you?" he asked, skipping around on his feet like a child. "Seeing as you're ghost hunters."

He looked around him as though what he wanted to say was for their ears only, but the courtyard was empty save for the three of them. Annie couldn't think of anything worse than having to hunt ghosts after the morning she'd had but Swift was all in.

"We'd love to, wouldn't we Annie?" he said, glee in his eyes.

"Great," Lewis smiled. "Meet me at the bar when you're done, and we'll head off."

Swift's glee vanished as soon as Lewis did.

"I get the feeling we join in here, or we get out," he said, lifting a chip coated in melted cheese and waggling it at Annie. "Sorry."

Annie grabbed the chip from his fingers and ate it quickly before he could protest.

"I say we get out then," she joked, but at the back of her mind a little voice was telling her to run.

LEWIS WAS SITTING AT THE WRONG SIDE OF THE BAR, coat gripped in his hand, as Annie and Swift brought in their empty dishes. They left them for the young girl who was now manning the pub and followed Lewis out onto the lane and back in the direction of Crow Cottage. Behind them, across the green, the school bell rang out and seconds later the young children ran out of the gates and onto the grass. The noise they brought with them was happy and loud. Screams of delight as they chased each other. Laughter as they ran around holding hands. The noise Annie knew well from her childhood, freedom as the school day ends and playtime starts.

"They're a great bunch of kids," Lewis said, looking back over his shoulder at the children.

"Did you go to the local school too?" Annie asked as they walked on past the green and up the hill towards the church.

"Yeah," Lewis affirmed. "My parents ran the pub before me, so I've always lived here. We had to travel to high school, but it's not far really. There's a bus that takes them these days, but I used to cycle. They don't know how lucky they are, not having to bike through thick snow."

Lewis laughed. The sound of children was soon replaced by the sound of birdsong as they walked up the hill away from the village green. Past the grave-yard and the church, Lewis cut through a narrow pathway and climbed over a stile that Annie hadn't noticed on her journeys back and forth to the cottage. Unsurprising really, given the hedge was growing over the wooden steps and blocked it from the lane. Lewis held back the foliage for Annie and Swift and they climbed over the stile onto a dirt track no wider than a single person. On their right was the Leylandii, on the left the graveyard as it surrounded the church, the spiked railing providing security all the way around too.

A figure, clad in black, stood in the side door of the chapel and raised a hand in greeting.

"Hello Vicar," Lewis shouted through the railings. "Just showing our newest guests the shrine."

Annie thought herself open minded, so she was a little embarrassed to acknowledge the shock at the vicar being female. Annie waved, recognising her as the woman who'd been sitting with Alf the dog walker last night in the pub. Her white hair stood out against the black cassock, and even from here Annie could see her deep wrinkles, the hunch to her shoulders, the way older people often look, too weary for this world.

"What kind of shrine are you taking us to that's not on church grounds?" Swift asked.

They broke out from between the hedge and the railings onto a meadow that swept away down behind the church. The valley below was bathed in sunlight, the yellow grass floated in the breeze then arched back up onto the hill beyond. A farmhouse was situated at the bottom of the hill, and Annie could see little white and brown dots of sheep on the far side of the valley.

"We needed somewhere to remember the family," Lewis said, walking around the back of the church. "And as their bodies were never found, we couldn't bury them on consecrated grounds because they weren't declared dead. We decided to celebrate them as near to the graveyard as possible."

"So you believe they're dead, then?" Swift asked. "That they didn't just run away."

Lewis looked at Swift as though he couldn't comprehend the question.

"Oh yes," he said, stopping at the foot of a large oak tree. "There's no doubt in my mind that they were all taken by the witch. She sacrificed the baby for our village and put the rest of the family to rest so they didn't have to bear the loss. We all had a price to pay, she reminded us of that."

"Who did?" Swift asked, and Annie could tell he was restraining himself. "The witch?"

"She made sure we all knew what had happened by sending a pestilence to the village." Lewis was wide-eyed. "And if you search the histories, you will see that wasn't the only time she'd brought a plague upon the village."

"Did anyone die?" Swift asked. "Anyone else I mean."

"No, she didn't need another sacrifice, she just wanted to show us who was in charge." Lewis folded his hands across his chest and nodded towards the tree.

Annie felt her skin crawl as the shrine came into view. The tree itself was like an alien, jutting out of the ground, its trunk thick enough to have to walk around it to see beyond its stockiness. Woven around the lower branches were tiny flags in what once must have been reds and blues, faded with age and dirt. They flapped about in the breeze like angry birds. Carved into the grey trunk was a tombstone, tall and narrow, the etches cut deep into the bark. RIP HARPER FAMILY stood bold at the top of the makeshift tombstone and all around the bottom of the tree were night lights strangely still in storm jars.

Annie stepped forward, her fingers primed to run over the carving when Lewis stepped in front of her, feet between the glass jars, his tongue darted out to wet his lips.

"We don't touch the tree," he said, his face only inches from her.

She could smell aftershave and fried food and stumbled back, a flashback of Harry making her stomach turn over itself with nausea. No one had been that close to her, not since he'd tried to take her life. Swift was by Annie's elbow in a second, discretely placing a hand under her arm and making sure she stayed upright.

"Sorry," Lewis said flatly, stepping back away from the tree. He didn't look sorry. In fact, Annie noticed the heat in his eyes at her reaction. He was enjoying this.

"Thanks for bringing us here, Lewis," Swift said, holding out his hand for the barman to shake. "We'll find our own way back. We were going to check out the walks behind the cottage anyway, so this is perfect."

Lewis looked between Swift and Annie, his eyes narrowing. He shuffled his feet on the dirt and rubbed at the back of his neck before taking Swift's offered hand. Annie knew he didn't want to leave them here alone. But it was public land, there was nothing he could do about it.

"Do you know where we can find Gerry?" she asked, trying to placate him, she really just wanted him to leave. "If you can get hold of him, we'd love to book one of his tours. Can you ask him to stop by the pub later?"

Lewis nodded. "Sure," he said, scratching at a spot on his lip until it bloomed red. "Are you okay to find your way back to the lane? I can show you if you'd like me to?"

A loud bang sounded out behind them. Gunshot? Annie spun around on her heels, grabbing Swift's arm. Lewis looked at her white knuckles, his face twisting into a grin.

"Don't be alarmed," he said, as though he was talking to a child. "That's just Alf and his bloody cars."

He broke into a laugh, walking back the way he'd led them. As he was disappearing into the small cut through, he turned back to face Annie and Swift.

"If the ghosts come to see you," he said. "Be sure to come back here and prey."

"What the?" Annie whispered when Lewis was out of sight.

"Two screws short of a toolbox if you ask me," Swift agreed.

"I'm not sure that's the saying, but I whole heartedly agree with you on that one."

Annie kept her back to the man-made shrine, not wanting to have to look at the unmoving flames or the crude carving. Beyond the meadow, in the courtyard of the farmhouse, Annie could see Alf as he tinkered with the shell of an old car held aloft on bricks.

"Let's take a walk," Swift said, offering his elbow.

Annie took it and they meandered away from the tree and the church, down the meadow to the valley. Free from the shade of the oak, the sun was warm on her head, relaxing and comforting, like sliding into a hot bath. A large rook flapped above their heads, cawing loudly, disturbing Alf from his car. He looked up and saw Annie and Swift, raising a hand in greeting.

"Hello again," he shouted, wiping his forehead with the back of a greasy arm. "How do?"

"Joe this is Alf," Annie said as they got closer. "Alf this is my... this is Joe."

Whenever Annie introduced Swift as her DI, people's perceptions of them immediately changed. They were here on holiday; she could drop the formalities.

"Nice to meet you, Joe," Alf said. "I'd shake your hand but..."

He held up his hands, black with oil.

"You too, Alf," Swift said, his eyes sweeping the farmyard. "No worries. Is this a working farm?"

Annie clocked what Swift was looking at. The locked-up sheds, the tarp covered cars blocking the stables. There was no mud or straw sweeping the paving.

"Not anymore, no," Alf said. "I'm too old for all that. No kids to pass it on to, so I sold most of my land off to neighbouring farms. I'm happy here with my cars."

He wiped his hands down his overalls, his head glistening with sweat. Grabbing a bottle of water, he took a swig.

"What're you doing down this way?" he said.

"Lewis was just showing us the Harper's shrine," Annie said, her own mouth feeling dry.

Alf rolled his eyes. "Was he now?" he said. "And?"

"Do you not agree with the village consensus?" Swift asked, leaning an arm on the chassis.

"Oh no, I do," Alf said, quickly, looking around. "It's just when you get to my age it's all a little bit, oh you know? I get tired of keeping up the pretence of being scared by the ghosts for all the hunters."

"We're hunters!" Annie balked, remembering that she'd told him where they were staying.

"You're no more ghost hunters than that there sheep." He pointed to a straggly brown sheep that was happily munching on the grass at the edge of its field. "I could tell that from a mile off. My guess is you're here looking for your sister and nothing else."

"Mim?" Annie asked, curious. "Are you sure you don't know her?"

Alf grabbed his toolbox and his water from the top of the car.

"Well, that's me done for the day," he said, heading around the car towards the farmhouse. As he neared Annie and Swift, he leant in towards them, the oil smell sticking in Annie's throat. The old man placed a gentle hand on her arm, his fingers warm and sticky on her skin. "I never met your sister. My guess is nobody in Ethlake would have met her and you're best to move on while you can."

Without meeting her eyes, he patted her on the arm and walked through the door to the farmhouse.

TEN

Annie and Swift looked at each other, stunned.

"Was that a friendly piece of advice or a threat do you think?" Swift asked her, tilting his head to the side.

"It was weird, is what it was," Annie replied, running her fingers over the propped-up hood of the old car. "He's quite obviously *not* finished here but couldn't get away fast enough."

They started off slowly, walking across the paved courtyard to the lane. Each of the large cart sheds had at least one car hidden under a tarpaulin. Some had two or three from the look of the shape the heavy-duty material made. Sandy the dog came trotting out the large, open shed at the back of the courtyard, his coat once again a shiny blonde.

Swift rubbed at the dog's head and gave Annie a little side eye smile.

"Is this your friend?" he asked, as they walked to the gate and crossed out of Alf's land to the lane.

Sandy stopped, an invisible barrier preventing him from leaving the farmyard. His tongue lolloped out of his mouth as he panted, a wave goodbye for the two off-duty officers.

"Yes," Annie said. "I like to think he's a good boy, really. But what if his shower of sh... pond water was a warning to me too. Like owner, like dog?"

Swift looked at Annie and started to cackle.

"A warning?" he said. "I think maybe you swallowed some of that algae."

The lane meandered around the back of the valley, cutting between two fields resplendent with woolly sheep before turning back on itself and leading up towards Crow Cottage. They walked in companionable silence, enjoying the birdsong and the occasional bleating from the sheep. As they crested the hill and started down towards the cottage, Annie noticed for the first time a little lean-to shed attached to the side of the stonework. The sun was so low in the sky, its windows flashed a burning red.

A warning? Annie thought again. *Why is everyone trying to get me to leave?*

She poked Swift in the upper arm to get his attention.

"Can we head straight back to the village?" she asked, not wanting to go inside again just yet. "See if there's anyone else around to chat to? School is out, and work, too."

She added, glancing at her watch.

"Sure," Swift replied, nonplussed. "Happy to."

They kept walking, on past the water tower and the church and down the lane to the village green.

Once again, the green was a hub of activity. A group of children, still dressed in the pinafores and grey trousers of their school uniform, were gathered around the May Pole, pretending to hold the ribbons while dancing in a weaving pattern under each other's arms. Their giggles could be heard from up the lane. A little away from them, two adults were arranging the pallets around the bottom of the bonfire, lifting them, and turning them over as though they were cartwheeling. Annie headed in their direction, recognising Gerry in their midst.

"Hi," Annie said, cheerily. "What's going on here? Can we lend a hand or two?"

Gerry stopped what he was doing, propping the pallet up against his hip. He brushed his hands together as though he'd just been eating crisps and held one out to Annie.

"Our resident ghost hunters," he said, smiling brightly. "I'm Gerry Needham, tour guide extraordinaire."

The other man working alongside him coughed loudly, but Annie heard a snigger there too. Gerry's smile didn't falter one bit. It stayed bright on his handsome face, dimples appearing in each cheek through his dark stubble. He reminded Annie of Superman up close, square jawed, muscular, twinkle in his eye. She was sure he could bat away a little ridicule with looks like those.

"Gerry," Annie said, shaking his hand. He didn't over-compensate and squeeze Annie's hand too hard, just a firm, definite once up and down and he let go. "Lovely to meet you. Everyone has been telling us to get in touch with you to book a tour."

"Old Lewis said you wanted to meet me today, and here I am," Gerry said. "Let's get you booked on. I've got a free slot tomorrow afternoon if you're brave enough."

Swift appeared behind Annie, a hot hand on her shoulder. Gerry looked at Swift and his hand and stepped fractionally back from the pair.

"Joe, this is Gerry," Annie said. "He's taking us on a tour tomorrow afternoon."

"Great," Swift replied, a little too loudly. "What's going on here?"

They all looked towards the bonfire as the younger man turned the last of the pallets then picked up a broom. He bent down and started poking the very base of the large structure with the wooden end of the long brush, hands gripped around the bristles.

"Hedgehogs," Gerry replied. "We move the fire around every day before we light it to make sure they don't start nesting. Duncan there is making extra sure."

Gerry rolled his eyes dramatically and the young guy dropped to his knees and pushed the broom handle into the unlit bonfire as far as it would go.

"Wouldn't want to burn the innocent now, would we?" Duncan said with a chuckle, sitting back on his haunches.

Annie recognised him as one of the teenagers who'd been sitting in the pub with the shop owner, Isla, only now she was nearer he was as much a teenager as Annie herself. He looked early twenties, same age as Mim. She thought better of asking him if he knew her sister in front of the others, but made a mental note to try and catch him alone later.

"And why are you burning *at all*?" Swift asked, removing his hand from Annie's shoulder and standing next to the huge pile of logs and twigs and pallets. He lifted one of the pallets away from the base of the structure, as though inspecting their work. Truth was, Swift probably had no idea how to build a bonfire, let alone inspect someone else's. "I thought May Day was all about celebrating the arrival of summer with dancing and singing and cake."

Duncan straightened up, pulling his shoulders back. He stood almost a head above Swift, who was over six foot himself.

"The founders of Ethlake were a marriage of Scots and Brits," he said, his eyes darkening. "It's tradition here to celebrate it both ways. We have the May Pole dancing for the lesser folk, and us real Celts have a celebration of Beltane."

It was Gerry's turn to snigger.

"Beltane?" Annie asked.

"The Celtic version of May Day," Gerry supplied, ignoring the angry stare from Duncan. "It's pretty much the same, except they dance around a big fire in masks and then spread the ashes over themselves and the fields to bless the crops."

"There's a lot of blessing going on here," Swift said. "What with the Witch and Beltane, why is Ethlake so in need of magic?"

Duncan scoffed. "You wouldn't understand," he spat, and Gerry placed a warning hand on his arm.

"Try me," Swift said, stepping up to Duncan.

Annie could practically smell the testosterone oozing from the three men. She rolled her eyes and intervened before someone got a black eye.

"Is it because of the witch you need to spread the ashes," she said, standing next to Swift and slipping an arm through his. She could feel the tension in his muscles.

"She's obviously a lot brighter than you are," Duncan said, his face relaxing.

Annie squeezed Swift's arm and she felt him relax too.

"Of course I am," she said, lightly.

"Sorry," Gerry added, taking a deep breath, and shaking his head. "You'll have to forgive us. It's a tense time of year here. The witch is always ripe at May Day, the start of summer brings with it droughts and famine and we know all too well that if the Witch isn't happy then our village will suffer. It was May Day when the Harpers disappeared."

"Does the witch take a sacrifice every year?" Annie asked.

Duncan and Gerry's eyes darted to each other and for a moment neither of them moved. It was Gerry who broke the silence.

"Let's not ruin all the fun for our tour tomorrow," he said, jovially, clapping his hands together before giving Swift a pat on the shoulder. "Tell me, young man, have you been on any other ghost tours around the UK? There's a few top notch ones I went on myself back in the day."

As Gerry was talking to Swift, Duncan snuck away, leaving the broom lying on the floor beside the pile of wood. Annie saw an opportunity and picked it up, running after the young man as he trudged across the green.

"Excuse me," she called after him. "You've forgotten this."

She could practically hear his eyes rolling in his head as he stopped and turned. To his credit though he'd thrown on a smile by the time he was facing her.

"Thanks," he said, taking the broom from Annie.

Annie didn't let go. She moved in closer before he had a chance to react.

"Did you know my sister, Mim?" she whispered. "She lived here last year, twenty-one. Looks like me."

A flash of recognition appeared on Duncan's face but was gone again as quickly as it came. Duncan looked around, they were far enough away from the bonfire, and the dancing children. In the middle of the green they couldn't be heard by the people in the shop or the pub either.

"If you know what's good for you, you'll stop asking about her." He hissed, pulling the broom from her hands so hard she felt her nail bend the wrong way. He pulled his face into a smile and added loudly. "Thanks for this. I'd forget my head if it wasn't screwed on."

Annie couldn't move. Her lungs burned, her heart was pounding frantically in her chest. He'd admitted he knew who Mim was. Not in so many words, but his warning was very different from the flat-out denial she'd met at every other turn. Why did he tell her to stop asking? Where was Mim?

Annie turned back to Swift, her throat thick with emotion. The sky was aflame with the sunset, blooming around the outline of the bonfire as though it was alight. Casting the rest of the green into shadows, places where secrets were made, and promises were broken. A shudder ran through Annie as she pictured masked figures dancing around the fire. Had Mim been with them last year? Had something happened to her on the night the Witch was said to bless or curse the village? Why was nobody talking to her? And why were those who did, warning her away?

ELEVEN

"ANNIE," SWIFT CALLED, WAVING FROM ACROSS THE green.

Annie cleared her throat and ran her palms over her cheeks, wiping away the tears.

She trotted over to him. Gerry was still talking and she didn't want to interrupt, but as he didn't seem to know how to take a breath between words, Annie figured she'd have to or they'd be listening to his stories until the end of their holiday.

"Gerry," Annie said, jumping in quickly.

"Annie," Gerry said, jumping back even quicker. "Joe here was just telling me about your brush with the plague last year. How exciting. That certainly has me pulling my socks up for your tour tomorrow. I can't compete with those awful plague doctor outfits, but I'll make sure I've got my best jacket on."

"Did he now?" Annie said, giving Swift a hard glare.

"I was just telling Gerry about what happened in the city, that's all," Swift added, obviously keen for Annie to know he didn't go into details. "About the deaths."

"Well hopefully there'll be none of those tomorrow, hey?" Gerry laughed. "I'll meet you at the May Pole at two? Make sure you're wearing suitable footwear."

He dothed an imaginary cap and strode off purposefully into the ever-darkening evening.

"Oh my god," Swift said, dropping his chin. "I thought he'd never stop talking. Thanks for rescuing me."

"Anytime," Annie replied. "Though you did call me over. Was there something you wanted to say?"

"Just *shut up*," he chuckled. "But that's kind of rude, don't you think?"

"Never normally stops you," Annie smiled.

"True, but we're playing a part here, aren't we? Not DI and psychotherapist, we're Annie and Joe." They started slowly towards the woods.

"Couple of ghost hunters or a couple sticking their nose in where it's not wanted, depending on who you talk to." Annie scuffed the toe of her flip flops on a mole hill, dry earth pattered over her feet. "Duncan practically admitted he knew Mim. Told me to stop asking questions. What do you think is going on here? Why are people so antsy? I'm not sure I believe they're all on edge because of the bloody witch."

They stopped where the tree line met the grass. On, past the thick trunks and dense foliage that let only a trickle of light seep through, the world looked like a different place to the welcoming, friendly feel of the village and the green. If Annie wasn't so stubborn, she could be easily scared by a dark wood and a witch's hut.

"I'm not so sure," Swift said, pulling back a low hanging branch and letting Annie go first. "Small places like this often have their own superstitions. Especially when, collectively, they've been subjected to a tragedy."

"So you think they believe in it all?" Annie asked, treading carefully. She was definitely not wearing the right footwear to be traipsing around in the woods in the dark. "Where are we going?"

"I think they need to believe in it all, yes." Swift said. He was right behind Annie, but she was having difficulty seeing him it was so gloomy. "Otherwise, the alternative is that there's someone going around killing people and hiding their bodies every year, or however frequently the witch is said to strike. I know what I'd rather root for. And to answer your other question, just a little further up, I think I can hear them."

Annie winced as a bramble got caught on her foot, piercing the top of her toes with a fierce sharpness. She bent down, carefully untangling the thorns from her skin, stabbing herself in the fingers in the process.

"Ow," she hissed, bringing her hands to her mouth and licking away the dots of blood that were blooming across her forefinger.

Just beyond the bushes, Annie could hear the chatter of what sounded like hyper, probably drunk women. She straightened up, letting Swift go in front.

"I don't know,' she said, still sucking at her sore finger. "I think I'd rather deal with something tangible. The witch is such an unknown entity, isn't she? Like, does she even live in the woods? Did she ever? Where did the rumours start?"

"Can she smell blood from a hundred yards away?" Swift added, and Annie could just about make out a grin through the darkness.

"It's alright for you," she said, whacking him on the arm. "You didn't have to run from the cottage and put on whatever footwear was nearest."

He scrunched up his face.

"The haunted cottage?" he asked, but before Annie had the chance to answer, Swift lifted another branch out of their way, and they almost stumbled upon the hen party who looked like they were creating a little seance of their own.

Sitting in a circle in the depth of the trees, the four women huddled around a storm lamp, not unlike the ones at the shrine. Each of them held a glow stick in one hand and what looked like a glass of Champagne in the other. The eerie, luminous light from the glow sticks gave the women a sickly pallor despite their spray on tans, and this evening they all wore velour tracksuits with what looked like diamanté names stuck on the fabric stretched over their boobs.

"Oh," Zoe exclaimed. Annie recognised her as the bride to be. "You startled me."

"Are you following us?" Jessica said, licking her lips at Swift. "Because you're more than welcome to."

The diamanté of the woman next to Jessica spelt out Megan, though they were stretched so far they might have said anything. Possibly-Megan let out a guffaw, slapping Jessica's thigh in delight.

"You'll scare the young man off, Jess," she screeched. "Here, are you joining us again?"

She directed her question to both Annie and Swift, and Annie liked her immediately. Swift shook his head.

"No," he said. "Not tonight. I don't want to crash your entire hen do. I just saw you heading this way and wanted to ask you something on the quiet, if I may."

The four women, Jessica, Zoe, possibly-Megan, and what read like Lucy, leaned towards Annie and Swift, their glow sticks wobbling in their hands sending shadows darting across the trees. Annie moved a little closer to the warmth from Swift's body, feeling his arm next to hers.

"The witch's hut," he whispered, dramatically. "Was there anyone living in it?"

Lucy, the only one of the women who hadn't yet spoken, drew her mouth into a smile.

"It's a creepy little shack a little further in the woods," she said, nodding her head towards where the hut must be situated. "But it's in ruins now, there's no way anyone could live there."

"Right," Swift replied. "In which case, we're going on Gerry's tour tomorrow afternoon. He's picking us up about two from the green. I would love it if you could creep around as quietly as possible when we're in the hut, then snap a few twigs or scrape your fingernails down the wood. Nothing too outlandish, just a little scare."

Jessica's eyes widened.

"Why?" she asked.

"It's Gerry's birthday." Swift ran his hands through his hair, a sure-fire sign he wasn't being truthful. "We want to give him a day to remember."

"Like ghosting the ghost man?" Lucy laughed.

"Exactly," Swift said, straightening back up.

The four women sat back on their blankets, grinning wildly.

"You're a hoot," Jessica said. "Of course we can. And we promise to be very discrete about it."

She zipped her fingers across her mouth, curling her lips inwards.

"Well ladies, once again it's been a pleasure." Swift held his hand in farewell. "Until tomorrow."

Annie waved goodbye and grabbed hold of Swift's arm as he turned to leave. The sun had fully set now and not even a glimmer of moonlight penetrated through the trees. But before they moved away from the women, Annie had a thought.

"I don't suppose Gerry told you how often the witch supposedly struck, did he?" she asked them.

Zoe tilted her head and watched as Annie stepped back to their gathering.

"Every nine years," the woman said, cautiously. "And there's no *supposedly* about it."

"Right, no, of course," Annie replied quickly, holding her hands up in defence. "Thank you. Thank you."

Swift hadn't moved so she grabbed his arm back and held on tightly as he led them back through the trees.

"You're a little tense, O'Malley," he said. "Worried about the witch?"

Somewhere up ahead a bird took flight, startled by their footsteps. The loud crashing noise as it flapped hard to break through the foliage made Annie's scalp crawl. She didn't want to make any loud noises. She didn't want to alert anyone to their presence. And Annie couldn't work out if that *anyone* included a witch that she didn't believe in or ghosts she knew weren't real.

"I'm just glad we're not visiting on a nine-year anniversary." Annie drew breath. "Because I am not sure the village folk wouldn't have us strung up on the bonfire, Wickerman style."

Swift whistled through his teeth.

"I know you've been through a lot, O'Malley," he said, squeezing her arm. "But you really don't trust anyone, do you?"

"I did," she said, quietly. "And look where that got me. Dating a serial killer."

They walked on in silence, the crunch of their feet on the undergrowth the only sound.

"But I do trust you," she added as the trees started to thin.

As the presence of the woods dissipated and the green welcomed them back, Annie felt a band of tension ping from her chest. She hadn't realised she'd been holding herself so tightly until she'd been freed. They walked across the grass and up towards the pond where the ducks were settling in for the night. And floating beside them, on a barely existent breeze came a song that made the hairs on Annie's arms stand to attention. A single voice, that of a young girl, her notes so finely tuned they whispered across the night with clarity, sang in perfect Gaelic:

Beannaich, a Thrianailt fhioir nach gann,
Mi fein, mo cheile agus mo chlann,
Mo chlann mhaoth's am mathair chaomh 'n an ceann,
Air chlar chubhr nan raon, air airidh chaon nam beann,
Air chlar chubhr nan raon, air airidh chaon nam beann.

TWELVE

WEDNESDAY

ANNIE AWOKE THE NEXT MORNING WITH A RIGOUR that was hard to shift. The clock beside her bed ticked gently. Glancing at it she saw that, although it felt like five minutes since her head hit the pillow, it was actually six hours and her body hadn't moved an inch in that time. No wonder she felt like the living dead. Groaning, Annie looked around the room, thinking perhaps *living dead* wasn't the best analogy.

There were no enticing smells wafting up through the cottage from the kitchen this morning. Pulling her dressing gown on and stretching out her crunchy spine, she made her way down the stairs and through the living room to the kitchen. There was a fresh pot of coffee waiting for her on the work surface and the door to the cellar was wide open. Grabbing a cup, Annie poured herself some hot coffee and took the stairs down into the echoey chamber under the cottage. Swift was already there, the photograph of the Harpers in his hands.

"Everything okay?" Annie asked, walking up behind him and looking down at the happy family.

"Morning, O'Malley," he replied. His eyes were red rimmed, hollow. "Hope I didn't wake you."

"No sleep again?" Annie asked, rubbing his arm. "That boiler has a lot to answer for."

Swift nodded.

"You know, I could have sworn that I heard a..." He stopped, grimacing. "Never mind."

"A what?" Annie asked, lifting the corner of the curtain that sat on top of the pile. It was heavy, good quality. Something about it made Annie's senses tingle, she couldn't work out what it was yet, but she filed it away to think over in more detail later.

Swift propped the picture back up on the pile and sighed.

"It was probably just tiredness, ignore me," he said, leaning back against the wall.

"Go on, try me," Annie prompted, knowing that whatever he told her, after the incident here alone yesterday, she'd believe him.

Swift picked at the skin on his thumb nail, his eyes narrowed.

"I think it was just after I'd drifted off to sleep," he said, his face paling. "Something woke me up. It must have done because I remember my heart was racing as though I'd had a fright. And before I'd really had a chance to come around... there was this voice, kind of, I don't know, humming."

A shiver ran down Annie's spine and the cellar dropped in temperature as though someone had walked in, bringing in the cold with them.

"Humming?" Memories of the singing girl fresh in her mind.

"Sort of," Swift replied. "I guess. I was still half asleep. It could have been the boiler."

"Last time I checked, boilers can't hold a tune," Annie said. There was something else bothering her about the cellar. She felt on high alert, as though ready to run or fight at any second.

Swift gave a short, sharp laugh.

"Yes, yes," he said, pushing himself up from the wall. His face looked slack, his jaw less of a line than normal. "I must have been dreaming, anyway, because I also saw a young girl."

Annie felt the floor of the cellar move away from under her feet. Her head swam. She reached out a hand to steady herself on the wall.

"Yeah," Swift said, quietly. "That's a bit like how I felt too. I wanted to see if there were any pictures of the whole family together, extended family maybe. See if I could find a picture of the young girl anywhere."

Turning on the spot, Annie leaned her whole body against the cool, damp plaster to stop it from buckling beneath her.

"When I was here alone yesterday," she said, feeling much less silly about admitting it now. "I heard someone too, I'm sure of it. I thought there was something watching me shower, but when I checked I was alone."

Swift's eyebrows shot skywards.

"Thanks for the warning, O'Malley," he said.

"We were warned by the whole bloody village," Annie scoffed. "And I told you right after it happened, but you took it as seriously as I did, because we *don't believe in ghosts.*"

"Shhh," Swift held a finger up to his lips. "You might anger them."

"I can't tell if you mean that or not," she replied. "But can we go back up to the cottage now, please?"

"Gladly." Swift was over by the stairs in a shot.

Annie took one last look around the airy room, the piles of belongings from a missing family notwithstanding, the space was eerie. And then she spotted something that made her misstep, trip over her feet in a rush to get to the stairs and safety. The Cabbage Patch doll was back on the pouffe, watching Annie with a stretched grin on its face.

Barely feeling the stairs under her feet, Annie rushed up them and slammed the cupboard door shut behind her. The windowsill was empty. Of course it was, the doll was back in the cellar where it belonged.

"Swift." Annie grabbed at his arm. "Did you take the doll back downstairs? Please say you did."

Swift placed a cool hand on top of Annie's, calming her.

"What doll?" he asked, rolling his lips.

"Oh god." Annie pulled out a chair at the little table and slumped into it. "The weird looking doll I brought up on Monday has somehow made it right back to exactly the same place I found it. And you're telling me it wasn't you who did it?"

Swift shook his head, pouring himself a cup of coffee. The cup Annie had taken down to the cellar with her was still there, she must have put it down somewhere to stop herself from dropping it. Though her memory of doing so was hazy enough to mean there was no memory at all. She dropped her head into her hands.

Swift gulped down his coffee and ran a hand over his stubble.

"I say we get dressed and get out into the sunshine," he said. "Things always seem better outside."

"Especially when the inside is haunted," Annie agreed. "I think I need to get away from Ethlake completely. Can you drop me off at the nearest town, please? There's something I want to check."

SWIFT PULLED INTO A PAY AND DISPLAY CARPARK AND found a space. The engine ticked over as it cooled, and Annie swung her door open.

"I won't be long," she said, jumping down from the car. "Meet you here in an hour?"

The hubbub of people milling around the high street made Annie feel like she'd popped a bubble and was back in real life. Ethlake had taken her in and quickly enclosed her in its magic. She felt as though time had slowed when she was there, like they were in a different realm with its own quantum physics. Yet here, in Southmallow, where the locals carried laden

ALDI bags and talked loudly into their mobile phones, was a breath of fresh air.

Following the directions on Google Maps, Annie wound her way past the early morning shoppers to the town centre. Southmallow Town Hall was housed in a prefab nineteen seventies building with a pebble dash exterior and a low squat roof. Not quite what Annie had been expecting, but as long as it held what she was after it could have looked like Doctor Who's Tardis for all she cared.

The man at the reception desk reminded Annie of a field mouse. His tiny frame barely reached over the counter and his dark rimmed glasses magnified his brilliant blue eyes. Annie smiled as she walked up to him, and he returned the smile, peeling his glasses from his face and wiping his brow with a handkerchief.

"Morning," he said, and she placed his accent at the west coast of Scotland and not the middle of Yorkshire.

"Hi," she replied. "I was wondering if you could point me in the direction of your archives, please?"

Placing his glasses on the desk, the man steepled his fingers together and twisted his lips.

"And what kind of archives were you after, young woman? he asked.

From the glowing skin and the lack of any errant greys, Annie could tell this man was a lot younger than her thirty-five years, but she didn't mind being called a young woman when she could get it.

"Electoral registers for the surrounding villages," she replied. "Just from the last few years, nothing too old."

"Follow me." He called over an older woman with tight white curls and a two piece to watch the reception and walked around the back of the desk and out into the hallway.

Annie followed him as he strode surprisingly fast down a grey corridor with one of those ceilings with the polystyrene squares that would blow away in a soft wind.

"Any village in particular you're after?" he asked, not turning around.

"Um." Annie wasn't sure she wanted to divulge that much, but she thought maybe the clerk might close off if she didn't. "Ethlake."

"Should have guessed," he said, muttering under his breath. "That's all anyone wants to know about."

"Oh, I'm not interested in the ghosts," she added, skipping a little as the man sped up around a corner. They must be near the back of the building now, Annie felt like they'd been walking for ages. "It's my sister, she lived there for a while and I'm trying to track her down."

He stopped abruptly at a door the same grey as the wall it was almost camouflaged. Pulling out a bunch of keys, he unlocked it and pushed it open for Annie.

"Right," he said, leaning in past her and flicking a switch on the wall. "Though it's not the ghosts people are normally interested in, it's the Harpers and the witch."

The room was windowless, the same grey as the rest of the building. It was like being inside a lego brick. Along the back wall was a row of metal shelving units, each holding stacks of box files.

"Most of the paperwork is held in storage," the man said, stepping into the room behind Annie. "But we keep the most popular here in the viewing room so we're not traipsing out to the units on a regular basis. And, luckily for you, Ethlake is our most popular destination. What year are you looking for?"

He motioned for Annie to sit down at the table, another grey throwback to her school days. The kind of table she sat at to eat chips and beans during lunch break.

"Maybe the last two or three to start with, please?" she said.

He headed to the nearest shelf and ran his fingers down the spine of the box files, stopping and lifting one down with great difficulty.

"Just out of interest," Annie said as he brought it to the table, popped it open and handed her three, thick, bound books. "What do people search when they're looking for the witch?"

The man did nothing to hide the way his eyes rolled at the question.

"Madeleine Cardeal," he said without missing a beat. "C-a-r-d-e-a-l. Would you like me to get her books?"

Annie shook her head, taking the bound files from the archivist with thanks.

"No, but what years would they be, if I *was* interested?"

"From nineteen-thirty-one." He walked back to the door; Annie had to twist in her seat to see him. "Don't remove any of the files, don't touch any of the files without asking, and no photographs. Come and find me when you're done."

He pulled the door closed behind him and Annie let out a breath. She felt like she'd been reprimanded by a headteacher and that had barely happened at school, let alone as a grown adult. Turning back to the bound files on the table in front of her, Annie found the earliest dated one and pulled it closer. Her heart was beating fast in her chest at the thought she might see her sister's name written on these pages. That she could see something tangible about where she'd lived, and not just rely on the word of a psychopath who had been trying to kill her.

Flicking through the pages, Annie found the Os from three years ago. She dared not look, so much was relying on her name being inked on these registers and if it wasn't, Annie would be all the way back at square one. Stealing herself, she ran a trembling finger down the page.

There she was.

O'Malley, Miriam.

An unexpected wash of emotion flooded through Annie. She felt her cheeks heat, tears pricked at her eyes and ran freely down her cheeks. Trying to swallow down the thick clod of tension in her throat, Annie moved her finger along her sister's details and read a small part of her history. Blinking away the tears, Annie read that, three years ago, Mim had lived in a small house on the outskirts of the village. Not so far out that she wouldn't have spent time on the village green, in the pub, and the shop. Why were these people all lying about having known her? Annie jotted down the address and moved to the next year. Same again. The next file was twenty-twenty, Annie flicked to the Os and ran her eyes down the list to the spot between Ollacourt and Osmaan. Nothing. No record of Mim. Annie pushed her hair back off her face and looked up at the grey walls. So Mim had left in twenty-twenty, two years ago. Counting up from eighty-four, Annie's fears were confounded. Mim had vanished from Ethlake during the year of the witch. She slammed the book shut, heart pounding in her neck. There was just one more thing left to check. Breaking two of the forbidden rules, Annie got up and walked over to the shelves.

THIRTEEN

"ANNIE O'MALLEY! HELLO STRANGER, HOW'S MY favourite psychotherapist?"

Annie could practically see Tink smiling down the phone. Her white, blonde pixie cut would be styled to look as though she'd just fallen out of bed and her lips would probably be painted a bright pink.

"Hi Tink," Annie replied, walking briskly back to the carpark to wait for Swift. "Lovely to hear your voice. I miss you guys. How's Page?"

The sounds of the police station were loud in the background. Their large, open plan office with the chatter of busy workers and the smell of station coffee felt quite appealing in comparison to where Annie was staying.

"Page is doing a Costa run," Tink replied. "He's keeping busy."

Tom Page was the youngest member of their MCU and was always getting the short end of the stick. Annie knew Tink would be looking after him while their boss was away galivanting.

"Can you do me a favour, please?" Annie asked, spying Swift leaning against his car with a take-away coffee of his own. She lifted her free hand in a wave.

"Anything," Tink replied.

Annie read out the details she'd written down for Madeleine Cardeal, the witch. Every address she'd lived at from the first entry in Ethlake in nineteen thirty-one to the last, in nineteen eighty-nine.

"Anything at all on this woman," she said, when she'd passed over the information. "Or associates."

"On it," Tink said. "And I can't wait to hear why both you and Swift are running secret stuff by Page and me when you're supposed to be on holiday."

Tink ended the call, so Annie pocketed her phone and made her way over to Swift.

The drive back to Ethlake was easy, Annie sipped at the drink Swift had bought her and wondered about what she'd read. What happened to Mim two years ago, and why did the witch leave Ethlake not long after the Harpers went missing, if she was supposed to bring a circular curse every nine years? Where did she go? And where are they both now? To his credit, Swift didn't prod her for details, he was quiet except for the occasional flurry of lyrics to a song he knew that cropped up on the radio.

They parked up at the cottage, just in time to take a quick stroll back down the lane to the pub. Gerry was waiting for them with a huge grin on his face.

"Well if it isn't today's lucky couple," he said, handing them both a lanyard. "Pop these on so I know you're part of my group."

Annie looked around for the rest of the group, or any other tourists hanging around that would mean Gerry needed to distinguish her and Swift from a flock of people. Apart from the family of ducks over on the green, the village was deserted. She slipped her lanyard over her neck anyway, reading the brightly coloured card hanging from the bottom. *Gerry's Ghost Games - scare if you dare.* Clocking Swift's amusement, Annie shook her head discreetly and he straightened his face.

"We're excited to be here, Gerry," Annie said, fiddling with the lanyard. "Thanks for fitting us in."

He moved about between Annie and Swift like an excited spaniel, a clipboard in his hand with a pen stuck under the clip at the top.

"You're welcome," he said. "It's an honour to take those guests staying at Crow Cottage on the tour. I don't normally do them over lunch time but seeing as how I was all booked up for the rest of the week, I wanted you guys to have the full monty visit. So to speak. I'm not actually going to get my kit off."

He winked at Annie and Swift breathed noisily with intent beside her. Gerry was oblivious as he set off towards the village green. Over at the far side, the children at the primary school were busily hanging brightly coloured decorations to the school fence. There were streamers and bunting, banners, garlands, and masks. They chattered loudly, running around in the playground as the teachers strapped the decorations to the iron railings with little helpers.

As they got closers, Annie could make out the shapes of the masks. Their long, ringed snouts protruding crudely below cut out eyes. They were painted in that haphazard way children with few fine motor skills coloured in.

"They'll be wearing those on Sunday," Gerry pointed. "Every year they make their own masks to wear to the celebrations. Aren't they wonderful?"

Wonderful wasn't the word on the tip of Annie's tongue. Creepy, unsettling, disconcerting had all sprung to mind. Why dress up the children like bulls on a day that celebrates the beginning of summer? Maybe it was a Beltane thing?

"We don't really have a lot of livestock around here to bless," Gerry said, watching Annie closely as she took in the masks. "So we bless the children and livestock together."

"Right." Annie nodded, with nothing to add that would keep Gerry onside.

Swift was surprisingly quiet as they made their way past the school and into the woods. He kept his head down, focussed on the ground under his feet, occasionally glancing at his watch. Unlike the way they'd come through the trees the previous night, this path was well worn with no overhanging thorns to grab at her skin. There was a lot to be said for health and safety. They passed by the hollow where the hen do had been drinking last night, washed out embers of their fire the only sign they'd been there. Annie remembered what Swift had asked of them and wondered how it'd play out.

"Madeleine Cardeal was a witch of the highest order," Gerry said from the front of their small group. "She grew up here in Ethlake and threw terror over the village for hundreds of years."

He stopped, twisting around on his feet to face Annie and Swift. Under the blanket of foliage, the darkness crept up on them and Gerry's face was awash with the shadows of the trees. The air smelt dank, like wet mulch left to rot, and bluebottles buzzed furiously around their heads.

"People come here in their droves, looking to find her. What they don't realise is," Gerry moved closer to them, his eyes hooded under lowered brows. "That although she's long gone, we're never free of her."

Something scuttled in the bushes behind them, making Annie jump. She swung her head around, but it was too shadowy to make anything out. Gerry nodded slowly, his face sagging.

"Every year she checks in on us, makes sure we're still reaping the rewards of her making." Gerry turned and carried on walking through the trees, shouting back over his shoulder. "If we're not, she'll make it known how angry she is."

The woods made way into a clearing. A circle of grass in the depths of the trees. In the middle, like the gingerbread house found by Hansel and Gretel, stood a tumble-down cottage right out of a fairy tale. The pitched roof sagged in the middle, green with age. The walls crumbled underneath. None of the glass remained the windows and the door hung from its hinges like a loose tooth. It was single story, quaint in its time, Annie imagined. The rickety picket fence around its perimeter was once white, but now looked as green as its surroundings, the uprights falling with age.

Gerry held out his hands towards the cottage, surveying the land.

"This was where she wreaked her terror," he said, quietly, a tremble to his voice. "So follow me inside if you dare."

Annie looked at Swift with a smirk, turning away quickly to collect herself when she saw he, too, was on the verge of bursting out laughing. Clearing her throat, she fell into step behind their guide and walked past the fallen fence to the cottage.

Though the trees stopped at the perimeter of the cottage grounds, letting light flood the small garden, inside was gloomy. The broken door swung precariously on its remaining hinge, rocking back and forth as they crossed the threshold. It opened straight into what must have been the kitchen, a dresser choked with dust stood against the wonky wall and a small sink with a curtain underneath was just below the little window. Gerry stopped to give his guests time to look around, consulting his clipboard with a pen torch.

"When did she leave?" Annie asked, trying to read the names of the cookbooks stacked on the dresser through the thick layer of dust. It was no good.

"Oh, she's never left," Gerry replied, earnestly. "If you were to come here after dark, you'd see her standing at her sink or the cooker. Look behind you."

Annie spun around, her skin fizzing with anticipation. Behind her was a small tabletop gas stove. Half expecting to see an old woman standing there stirring a pot, Annie was relieved to see the stove was as covered in dirt as the rest of the room.

"Okay, then," Annie said, trying a different tact. "When did she leave in body?"

Gerry looked at her as though she had two heads and moved on through to the next room.

"Stop ruining his tour," Swift whispered, grinning.

"What?" Annie mouthed back, innocently.

The next room was the same size as the kitchen, and just as grubby. An old wooden rocking chair sat in front of a wood fire; apart from this, the room was empty. Another two doors led to a bathroom that would have looked better placed in an old outhouse, and a bedroom. Annie chose the bedroom. The pink eiderdown covering the mattress looked as though it would plume with dust if she even looked in its direction. Moving carefully down the side of the bed, careful not to touch anything, Annie reached the wooden table at the bed head. It looked as though there had been a volcano eruption, the dust like the settling of ash rendered everything as mounds of grey. Though she could make out what looked like the shape of a hairbrush, a glass, and a book.

Quickly checking over her shoulder, Annie ran a finger down the spine of the paperback, covering it back over with dust as best she could afterwards. She inched back out of the room and went to join Swift and Gerry by the unlit fire.

"And sometimes people can hear the creaking of this chair if the wind is blowing in the right direction," Gerry said, his eyes wide.

"Goodness," Swift replied. "That must be scary?"

Gerry nodded. "We're taught from a young age to respect the witch and her magic here in Ethlake. No-one else wanted to take on the tours as they were all too scared, so it fell to me to continue on with this role. *What was that?"*

Gerry's eyes grew even wider, the whites reflecting the light from the pen torch still focussed on his clip-board. Outside Annie could hear the creaking of a heavy branch and rustling of leaves. Swift twisted his head to see out the window and started creeping towards the empty panes.

"Shhh," he said, holding a hand up to still the others. "There's something out there."

Gerry let out a high-pitched whimper that made Annie's hair stand on end.

"What have I done wrong?" Gerry cried as softly as he could. "I'm sticking to the itinerary just as I do every tour."

Swift flapped his hand to try and get Gerry to stay quiet. Outside the window the heavy branch creaked and squealed until, with the sound like a human child crying, it broke off, landing somewhere in the woods with a thud. The stillness that followed felt like a vacuum. Until, with a blood chilling fear, a low echoing chuckle filtered through the trees.

Gerry dropped his pen torch and clip board with a clatter that made Annie jump. He fled out through the kitchen, and they heard his footsteps crunching through the trees until all was quiet again.

"Thanks, guys," Swift called out the window. "You're all angels."

Annie felt sick to her stomach.

"Did you get the reaction you wanted, Swift?" she asked, her voice barbed. "Was it really fun to scare poor Gerry half to death?"

Swift picked up the clipboard and pen, clicking off the light and attaching it to the top of the board.

"You can't ask people whether they believe in something without them a) lying to you or b) getting all precious about it." Swift was looking at the itinerary on the board. "And Gerry here has just proved to us that he is completely and utterly taken in by the idea that a witch lived or lives here and is placing a curse on the village."

"And you don't believe that?" Annie asked.

"No," Swift said, looking up from the clipboard and right into her eyes. "I don't. You?"

Annie shook her head. "Not unless witches read Danielle Steel books, no. But it was still going a bit far scaring Gerry like that."

They traipsed back out of the cottage and through the woods. Not hearing the creaking of the door as it swung closed behind them.

FOURTEEN

THURSDAY

ANNIE PULLED HER TOWEL AROUND HER AND STEPPED out of the shower. The small en-suite had a fine coating of mist in the air and the tiny fan was chugging away, working hard but not very effectively. Unable to see herself in the bathroom mirror, Annie threw open the door to the bedroom to use that one instead and came face to face with Swift.

"Joseph Richard Swift," Annie yelled, pulling her towel tighter. "I'm going to report you to the local police for being a Peeping Tom!"

Swift threw his hands up in front of his face and tried to back out of the bedroom, bumping first his Achilles heel on the corner of the bed, then his funny bone on the door frame.

"Ouch," he hissed, dropping his hands from his eyes to rub his sore bits, hopping madly, and swaying from side to side. "I'm not a Peeping Tom. I didn't know you were in there."

"Thief then?" Annie asked, a wide grin spreading over her lips at Swift's red-faced embarrassment.

"Nope," he said, peeking out a scrunched-up eye at Annie's amusement. "You joker."

Annie gave a shrug. "What can I say?"

"I thought you were naked," Swift laughed. "God, that would have been a fright."

Picking up the nearest item to hand, Annie lobbed yesterday's socks in Swift's direction. Narrowly missing his head.

"What you up to then?" she asked, blowing a wet lock of hair that had fallen free of the towel on her head. "If you're not trying to sneak a peek at this?"

She loosened her towel off and started pulling it away from her body. Swift threw his hands up to his face again.

"STOP!" he yelled.

"I'm kidding, jeez." Annie scrunched her nose and threw a smile at him, tucking the end of the towel safely around itself. "But what are you doing, really?"

Swift plonked himself down on Annie's bed, running a hand through his own unruly hair and down a heavily bristled chin.

"I've come to borrow your brush again, if that's okay?" He looked down at his fingernails. "And to ask if you've maybe taken my razor, you know, for your… bits and pieces."

Annie almost choked on her own spit.

"My bits and pieces?" She giggled.

"I don't mind, of course," Swift added, his cheeks growing even redder. "I just need to sort out my face and I need it back, please?"

"Oh, Joe," Annie sat down next to him on the bed, her towel shifting across her thighs. "My beautician would have a fit if I started shaving between waxes. And can you imagine taking a razor to your face that had just attacked my bits and pieces? Not nice."

She patted his knee and searched her bedside table with her eyes for the hairbrush. It wasn't there.

"You've still got my brush, I think," she said, not wanting to bend down and check under the bed while Swift was in the room and she was dressed only in a towel. She didn't really want him to see her naked.

"And I'm sorry, but I'm not the one who has your razor."

Goosebumps started to prick up her shins, dotting her thighs like a recently plucked chicken.

"That's weird," Swift replied, echoing her thoughts.

Weird, the word of the holiday so far.

"Have you checked everywhere?" she asked, feeling the cold drips from her hair tickling down her bare shoulders.

"Yeah."

"Like, properly checked, not just swung your eyes around the room and decided you can't find them?"

Swift tilted his head and raised an eyebrow.

"I'm a detective," he said, pointedly. "I know how to find… stuff." He got up off the bed, looking down at Annie. "But I'll just go and have another look, just in case."

Annie shut the door behind him, reminding him to knock next time. She towel dried her hair and brushed through it the best she could with her fingers. It knotted around itself like seaweed but it was the best she could do without a brush. Throwing on some jeans and a T-shirt, Annie went down the stairs to get some coffee. She found Swift in the kitchen; he was on all fours with his head stuck in the cupboard under the sink.

"I know I said to look properly," Annie said, leaning over him and pouring herself a cup from the jug. "But I'm almost one hundred percent sure that your razor and my hairbrush are not under the kitchen sink."

She perched on one of the chairs at the little table and waited for Swift to emerge.

"I thought I heard something," he said, rubbing at the back of his neck. "Maybe I'm going mad."

Annie sipped at her coffee, her mind whirring as Swift came to sit with her.

"It's weird," she said, digging at the table with a fingernail. "This village seems stuck in the dark ages with its curses and witches and sacrifices. They're putting on a show though, aren't they?"

Swift nodded.

"That's the impression I get too," he said.

"So where do we go to get the real deal?" Annie asked. "Where will these villagers be themselves and not try to scare us with witch stories or ghosts?"

Swift turned his attention to the window, the courtyard garden blooming with blues and purples of the Allium and the Lupins. A bird bath with a stone robin perched on the rim was in need of a top up and there was a small shed right at the bottom that was painted in a rich teal. The garden didn't get much sunlight, but luckily there were the fields and the village green to run around in instead, free from the shadows cast over the courtyard.

"I think I have our answer," Annie said, pointing at the glass. "A shadow cast."

Swift wrinkled his nose.

"The water tower?" he asked.

Annie slumped her shoulders.

"No, *detective inspector*," she said, eyes back on Swift, pouting at him. "The church."

WALKING INTO THE CHURCH WAS LIKE WALKING INTO A different season. Instantly the tips of Annie's fingers and toes felt like ice and the warmth of the late April sunshine stopped at the door, waiting patiently for Annie and Swift to finish their business and leave. Their footsteps echoed on the tiled floor, rattling around into the eaves, past the stained windows with angels and bishops and other famous icons which Annie didn't recognise.

"This place is huge," Swift said, his voice booming around the expanse.

"For a small village, it's certainly on the large side." Annie walked up the nave, past the long aisles on either side which housed hard wooden pews and leather-bound bibles.

The alter lay ahead, past where the cross of the building spread on both sides. She wasn't a religious person, with everything that had happened in her childhood and the possibility of a father who'd kidnapped her sister and joined a cult, religion was a subject as sore as politics. Annie believed that nothing good could ever come from talking about it. But when faced with a building like the one she was standing in, Annie could see what attracted people to it. There was a sense of calm around her, a stillness, a feeling that everything would be okay. And though the air was cold, it wasn't aggressively so. More a nod to Annie to remain respectful.

"I wondered when you'd come." The vicar appeared through a small door to the left of the alter. She bowed her head to Annie, her white hair cut short to her head. Something about her face felt familiar, perhaps it was the way of the church, familiarity helps to sooth.

"Vicar," Annie said, all at once feeling like she'd done something wrong. "Sorry, I hope we're not intruding?"

The vicar gave a small laugh devoid of humour and motioned to the pews where Swift was hovering. He'd not made it very far into the building.

"There is no intruding when it comes to The Lord's house," the vicar said, her movements slow and pained. "No matter how uncomfortable it makes you feel."

Gripping the back of a wooden pew in her hands, the vicar stopped to catch her breath before hobbling on towards Swift. Under her heavy cassock, Annie noticed how thin the woman's legs were, how the tendons in her neck stuck out like the struts of her umbrella. She was nothing but skin and bones.

"Vicar," Swift said, nodding once.

"Young man," the vicar replied, dropping to the pew in front of Swift so suddenly, Annie thought she'd not really meant to. "Please don't worry. The Lord does not judge and is all forgiving."

Swift paled and sat down on the row opposite, his elbows resting on his knees. Annie felt like she'd walked into the middle of a conversation already happening between the vicar and Swift. She quickly took a seat on the row in front of the vicar, twisting her body so she was facing the old woman, and waited for them to finish.

"How are you enjoying your *holiday?*" the vicar asked, coughing out another hollow laugh.

"How can you tell?" Annie asked in return.

Dark circles under the old woman's eyes looked like she'd painted them there with stage make-up, but the steeliness of her gaze was authentic enough.

"Young lady, I have been around long enough to know police officers when I see them."

It was Swift's turn to cough. He tilted his head, shaking it slowly.

"We're not here as police," he said, as if surprised by her astuteness.

"No judgement from me, either," the vicar replied.

Annie shifted on the hard wooden bench, it wasn't quite deep enough to get comfortable on sitting sideways, but she imagined it wasn't much better sitting straight on, either. Her hip bone ached, and her ankle had started to throb. It had been months since the healed break in her ankle made itself known.

"Honestly," Annie said, holding her hands up. "We're here as a sister and a friend. We might not be ghost hunters but we're not looking for trouble."

The vicar gave a smile that seemed to use up a lot of energy.

"It's a nice change," she said, opening her arms out to both Swift and Annie. "To have visitors who haven't come to ask me twenty questions about the witch or the Harpers or even the ghosts."

"Do you get a lot of those?" Swift asked.

She sighed wearily, lifting her arm, and pulling a bottle of water from a small cross-body bag. She twisted the lid with knuckled fingers and took a sip. The water brought a pinkness to her cheeks and she straightened up a little on her pew.

"It's all I get," she said. "Apart from Sunday service, my whole parish life revolves around answering questions about something that happened an age ago."

She opened her mouth, her eyes narrow, but must have changed her mind about what she was about to say. Closing it again, the vicar placed her hands together in her lap and took a deep breath.

"Isn't all religion about what happened an age ago?" Swift asked, and Annie winced. The vicar took it in her stride, probably used to being heckled by non-believers.

"Religion isn't just about God," she replied, stoically. "It's about a community, a place of belonging. It's about feeling safe and doing your best for yourself and others."

Swift looked suitable reprimanded.

"Sorry," he said, holding his hands up. "I was just being facetious."

"You look like you've had enough of being asked about the witch?" Annie probed, giving Swift a steely look. "What do the rest of the villagers think? Are they as fed up as you are?"

A rattle of the church door interrupted the vicar's reply. They all turned to look as the door burst open and a dozen young children holding hands in pairs marched into the space, bringing with them a swathe of warm air and a bouncy chatter.

"Don't listen to the moanings of an old woman," the vicar said, holding on to the back of the pew with shaking hands and pulling herself to her feet. "We're indebted to the villagers here in the parish and we wouldn't have such a wide variety of visitors without a little tale to tell them."

She bowed her head to Swift and made her way towards the children who'd been joined by an harassed looking young woman. They watched the vicar hold onto the tops of the pews, her thin legs like matchsticks that had already been burned to a crisp and threatened to snap at any moment. The children gripped tightly to carrier bags stuffed full of streamers and bunting and on the word of their teacher they ran off in all directions, their decorations flying behind them, bull faces wherever Annie looked.

FIFTEEN

"I don't know about you, O'Malley," Swift said as they walked out into the bright sunshine. "But I want to go and collapse on the sofa and drink a beer. I'm going to need a holiday to get over this holiday."

Annie felt the cold of the church seep out of her bones and held her face up to the sunshine.

"I know," she replied, her eyelids burning bright red. "Trust my sister to live in a place with a history more interesting than our own."

"You're maybe more alike than you know." Swift started back up towards the cottage.

Annie blinked the dots from her eyes and followed after him, feeling a surge of pride for her long-gone sister. Exhaustion was a heavy weight on her shoulders too, but Annie wasn't quite ready to go and sit down just yet.

"Do you fancy having another look at the shrine on the way back?" she asked, tilting her head towards the narrow gap between the church and the hedge. "Just a quick one."

The dark circles etched under Swift's eyes made him look like he was a few weeks out of a boxing match, but she broke out the pleading face and he gave in pretty quickly. They climbed over the style and dropped down onto the narrow path, walking up towards the shrine that Lewis had shown them a few days ago. Branches from the hedge dragged against Annie's arm like fingers even though she was as near to the iron railings of the church as she could be. Speeding up, Annie broke out from the pathway onto the field with a sigh of relief. The meadow in front of her dropped away into the valley, Alf's cars at the bottom, all lined up across the farmyard like toy trucks.

"Come on then, O'Malley," Swift said, marching in front of her. "There's a bacon sandwich with my name on it calling me back to the cottage."

Annie's stomach gave a low rumble and she quietened it with her hand. Swift kept moving, disappearing behind the back of the church railings. Annie skipped to catch up, holding on to her hair as a gust of wind whipped around the open space and blew her side-ways, away from the church, away from the shrine. Strands of hair flew into her face, tangling in her eyelashes. She couldn't see the field in front of her, Swift was an apparition of reds and blacks, the solitary tree loomed over him. The wind blew across the back of her bare neck, a gentle kiss of air now, crawling fingers up into her scalp. She brushed her eyes free of hair, pulling out a hairband from her pocket and tying it up in a top knot.

"That was weird," she said, stepping tentatively over to Swift by the base of the tree.

"What was?" he said, looking at her.

"The wind," she replied. "Almost blew me over. Seemed to want to stop me looking at the shrine, it was trying to blow me down the hill."

"Didn't feel it," Swift said. "And I'm not sure wind has the means of ulterior motive. Is all this talk of ghosts getting to you?"

Her mum always used to say she soaked up the atmosphere of a place like a sponge, and this was true of Ethlake. She pouted and turned her attention to the tree. The bunting was still, not moved by the winds. The candles sat unlit, their black wicks drooping in hardened wax.

"He must have planned to bring us here when he did," Annie said, thinking of how *alive* the shrine had seemed with the flickering candles and the fairy lights.

"I was just thinking the same thing," Swift said. "But also, the family went missing nearly forty years ago. How is all this still looking so new?"

"And where are the shrines to the other sacrifices?" Annie added, her mind whirring with all the questions.

They closed in on each other, arms almost touching. The air seemed to still and Annie thought she could hear the joyful cries of the children in the church behind the tree. But there was something else there too. A scrunch of leaves. The sound of footsteps on gravel. The hissed voices of two people not wanting to be overheard.

Annie held up a finger to her lips, keeping Swift in silence.

"What do you want?" The first voice said. They must be in the churchyard, right at the back past the grave-stones. The railing stopped short behind the tree that was hiding Annie and Swift.

It was Isla, the shop owner.

"We need to do something," the other voice replied. This one was Lewis. "They can't stay here."

"We've tried that before, remember?" Isla said. "And look at how that turned out? Anyone know where *she* is now?"

Annie heard the crunch of gravel and a muffled cry.

"Stop it, Isla," Lewis growled. "You know I had nothing to do with that. All I'm saying is that we need to move them on."

"Get. Your. Hands. Off. Me," Isla replied, her voice low, threatening. There was another scuffle and Lewis let out a yelp. "You have no idea what I'm capable of. They are only staying a few more days, we keep our heads down and get on with things."

"But this week, of all weeks?" Lewis sounded desperate. Footsteps in the gravel faded away as someone left the secret meeting. "Isla, please. Shit."

Annie and Swift waited until Lewis had followed after Isla before stepping out from the cover of the tree.

"Well that was interesting," Annie said, moving quietly towards the pathway back to the lane. "Do you think the *they* Isla and Lewis were talking about is us?"

"Most definitely." Swift followed her. "But what are they worried we're going to do?"

"Or are they worried *for* us?" Annie asked, checking the lane both ways before climbing back over the style. "And do you think the other person they mentioned is Mim?"

Swift jumped down beside her and they walked back up the tarmac towards the cottage.

"Maybe," he said. "But don't let's jump to conclusions. We still need to hear back from Tink and Page about the villagers, maybe they'll come up with another person who's recently left Ethlake."

"Maybe." Though even as she was saying it, Annie didn't believe.

———

THE COTTAGE GREETED THEM LIKE AN OLD FRIEND. She'd soaked up the sun's rays and the living room was warm and inviting. Annie slumped down onto the sofa under the stairs, her legs pounding from walking up hills that were non-existent back in Norfolk. Swift returned from the kitchen with two bottles of beer, handed one to Annie, and took his usual seat on the other sofa. With the sun streaming through the window, pooling light on the stone floor, Annie felt if she closed her eyes, she might well fall asleep.

Instead, she sipped her beer and tried to engage her thoughts about the last four days in Ethlake.

"I feel like we're in the middle of a case and this is our incident room," she said, curling her legs under her on the sofa.

"Okay," Swift said, stretching out straight along his sofa, propping his head on a cushion. "So let's forget about Mim for a second." He held a hand up to Annie. "Not forget, forget, I think she plays a part in this too.

But let's forget the reason we came here and think about Ethlake and its villagers."

Annie leant her head against the back of the sofa, sipping again at her beer. It was going down rather nicely, though without any food in her stomach she could feel the pull of alcohol already taking hold.

"We've got a witch with a history," she started. "A missing family. And a village with a lot of secrets."

Swift nodded.

"But what we've actually got is a witch who supposedly has been around hundreds of years," he said. "A witch who lives in an old run-down cottage in the woods. Who makes sacrifices every nine years to maintain the status quo of the village.

"And checks on how well they're all doing every year?" Annie added. "

"Yep. But then in the eighties, the Harpers go missing. Everyone puts it down to the witch and her sacrifices, even though there are no other cases of missing people here before or after, that we know of."

"Apart from possibly Mim?"

"Apart from your sister, yes."

"I looked up the witch's details too, while I was at the town hall, and she lived here until a few years after the Harpers went missing," Annie said, stretching her legs out in front of her to get the blood flowing again. She turned on the sofa so she could see Swift. "This cottage is where the family used to live and is supposedly haunted. By the family? By some of the family? By others who've been sacrificed?"

"And don't forget the belongings left in that dingy cellar." Swift finished his beer and put the bottle on the floor beside him. "As though the family may one day return home."

"So are they missing or sacrificed?"

The silence that followed Annie's question was filled with the sounds of spring. A bumble bee, bird song, the gentle bleating of nearby sheep. She felt her eyelids get heavy and blinked a few times to wake up a little.

"Then we have the villagers." Swift's voice made her heart race, she must have been on the edge of falling asleep. "Families who've lived here for years, whose children are now running the place. There's Isla at the shop, her children looked like teens, maybe they'll take over from her. It's a thriving little business by the looks of it. There's Lewis in the pub he inherited from his parents, again, very busy with visitors. Both of them are worried about our presence. By us or for us, who knows? But they both have a majority say in how the village is run, so it would seem."

"Alf and his dog and his farm and his cars," Annie said. "He wanted to stay here so much he sold off a load of land to be able to do so."

"And the vicar who looks like she's about to drop dead any second," Swift added, a little humour in his voice. "Why hasn't she upped and retired yet? Does the village hold on to people, or are they too scared of the witch?"

"Gerry was obviously scared of her," Annie said, remembering the way the young tour guide had run away from the cottage. "And he said that he was only doing the job because no-one else was brave enough."

"There's an undercurrent of distrust in people who come to Ethlake," Swift said. "Unless they're ghost hunters. Which brings us to your sister."

"Is she a ghost hunter?" Annie asked.

"Precisely," he replied. "And why are they all denying her existence?"

"Maybe she's the new witch," Annie laughed, closing her eyes to the sun as its rays peaked beneath the stairs and blanketed her with warmth.

WHEN HER EYES JOLTED OPEN WHAT FELT LIKE moments later, the sun was long gone. Annie groped around in the dark for her phone but came up empty handed. A blanket covered her legs, probably a parting gift from Swift after she'd fallen asleep, but Annie still shivered. She shifted up on the sofa, her neck screaming in pain where she'd been laying curled around her arm. Slowly, her eyes adjusted to the low light, but with the curtains pulled, blocking out the stars, and no lamps switched on, the room was like a black hole. All Annie could focus on were outlines, the door frame, the stairs above her head. A person? The breath was sucked from her lungs, her hair standing to attention on her arms. Stars flickered in the corner of her vision, stippling her limited view. The outline of shoulders was clear.

Above her head, Annie heard the creaking of floor-boards. *Please be Swift, please come and check on me.* But the figure in front of her didn't move. Blood pumped in her ears, annoyingly blocking out any small noises that she could rely on to keep her safe. The shuffle of a footstep or the hitched breathing from the stranger. But through the sounds like rushing water, Annie heard the solitary voice of a young child singing the song of Beltane once again.

SIXTEEN

FRIDAY

IT WAS AS THOUGH TIME STOOD STILL. IN THE blackness, Annie felt her head swim, full of the child's voice and the icy terror it brought with it.

BEANNAICH, A THRIANAILT FHIOIR NACH GANN,
MI FEIN, MO CHEILE AGUS MO CHLANN,
MO CHLANN MHAOTH'S AM MATHAIR CHAOMH 'N AN
CEANN,
AIR CHLAR CHUBHR NAN RAON, AIR AIRIDH CHAON NAM
BEANN,
AIR CHLAR CHUBHR NAN RAON, AIR AIRIDH CHAON NAM
BEANN.

The voice was so clean, it echoed around the cottage, piercing her ears. Annie had no idea what the words meant which made them even more terrifying.

The figure hadn't moved, transfixed by the song spiralling down the stairs. What was he doing? Was this prowler as scared by the song as Annie? With trembling hands and legs that felt as though they were boneless, Annie slid from the sofa onto the floor. Noiselessly, she tiptoed across the living room, barely daring to breathe. If he looked this way, Annie had nowhere to hide and nothing to do but attack with her bare hands.

The singing grew louder, the same words repeating over and over again. Annie wanted to rip the ears off the side of her head. The lyrics grew clearer as Annie moved to the bottom of the stairs. Her eyes adjusting more to the darkness. Her heart was beating so hard she could feel it all though her body, her neck, the backs of her knees, her arms, they all throbbed with the rate her blood was being pumped. She lifted her arms, drew back her right hand and curled her fist into a ball the way her Mum had taught her when she was just a child. Thumb out, loose shoulder joint, feet a hip width apart. With the element of surprise, Annie had just one attempt to subdue this creep.

Three.

Two.

One.

Annie lunged forwards, throwing her punch towards the ribs of the figure in the hopes that she could wind him. Her fist hit fabric and she braced herself to take the impact. But she kept going, her hand passing through the figure as though they were a ghost. Annie stumbled, with nothing to take her weight, the momentum of her punch dragged her forwards until she hit the floor fist first, with a thud.

The pain shot up her wrist. Annie cried out, rolling over onto her backside. Above her the figure was swaying gently from side to side, illuminated now by a soft white light from up the stairs. It was Swift's coat hanging over the upright lamp.

"You idiot," Annie said to no-one but herself.

Relief flooded rapidly though her, her arms and legs tingled with pins and needles. Shaking her head, Annie got up from the floor, brushing herself down and checking her wrist. She could flex it without too much pain, and her fingers all wiggled when she tried them. She looked back up at the stairs and listened to the song with a renewed sense of calm. It was quite beautiful, like the first few words of 'Once in Royal David's City' sung at Christmas time. Swift must have the radio playing.

Her watch showed the time as almost four in the morning, so maybe he'd accidentally left it on and fallen asleep. The stairs creaked under her feet as she climbed them, wanting her own bed after the lumpy sofa. She rounded the top and onto the landing, the glowing white light brighter here, pouring from around the sides of Swift's open door, the song louder and more pronounced. Tiptoeing so as not to wake him, Annie crept into his bedroom to turn off whatever he'd left running but when she peeked around the open door, she saw him sitting up in bed, wide eyed staring at something across the room. Annie's eyes followed his and she stumbled backwards, unable to stop herself from crying out. There, at the very back of Swift's bedroom, near the noisy airing cupboard was a young girl, mouth open in song, her whole body glowing white like the moon.

"Run, Annie," Swift yelled, scrambling out of bed. "Go, go."

He scuffed along the floor, hands pulling at the floorboards as if that would make him go faster. Annie spun around, her whole body alive with fear, and ran as fast as she could back down the stairs. Swift pounded down behind her, whimpering like a Labrador, flicking on every light switch he passed by. The living room lit up like a fair ground ride, main light, lamp, porch light, side lights. But this did little to sooth Annie's racing heart as she kept running through to the kitchen, slamming the door shut behind Swift as he barged past her.

She hit the switch in the kitchen and the strip lights buzzed on, casting them in a sickly yellow glow. The cellar door was shut tight, but Annie threw a chair against it anyway, sitting down on it and dropping her head into her hands.

"What was that?" she asked, as soon as she'd caught her breath. "What the hell was that?"

Swift had slid down the cupboards next to Annie and was sitting with his head against the sink. His skin shone with sweat, looking like baker's dough under the hard lights.

"I was fast asleep." Swift's voice shook. "Something must have woken me, a crash I think, but who knows. And I could hear this awful singing. I thought you'd turned on the TV but when I opened my eyes..." He took a breath, coughing as it hitched in his throat. "I thought the village were joking about the cottage being haunted to make people want to stay here. But..."

Annie looked up from her hands.

"You think what we've just seen was a...?" She couldn't say it out loud. It was too stupid.

"Shh." Swift held a finger up to his lip and once again Annie felt her body tense, primed for what was to come. "Listen."

She listened, but all she could hear was the dripping of the tap above Swift's head and her own heartbeat.

"I can't hear anything," she whispered.

"Exactly," Swift said, shifting to his feet. "The singing has stopped."

He walked to the door and held his ear there, his eyes sweeping back and forth across the room, always alert.

"It's definitely stopped," he said, turning the door handle.

"What are you doing?" Annie cried, not ready to leave the safety of the kitchen.

"I don't know," Swift pulled the door ajar. "I can't stay in this room though, waiting for it to glide down the stairs and float through the bloody door."

That wasn't what Annie had been expecting. Her skin prickled. She knew Swift hated being out of control, but going back out there already? It wasn't sane, was it?

"Well for goodness' sake," she said, feeling the threat of vomit gurgle up her throat. Swift shook his head and tiptoed out into the living room. "Don't leave me here on my own."

She scrabbled off the chair and followed. Swift was right, the singing had stopped. Even the white glow from up the stairs was gone, though that could be because the living room was glaring with light.

"Put the kettle on, O'Malley," Swift called back over his shoulder. "There's no way I'm going back to sleep. I could use a coffee."

Through the gap in the curtains, Annie could see the sun starting to rise in the sky, taking with it the fears of the night. Everything seemed better in daylight. She threw the curtains open and went to make a pot of coffee.

"All clear," Swift said, as he took the cup from Annie and settled onto the sofa.

"You went back up there?" Annie asked, wrapping the blanket around her shoulders.

"No," he replied, smiling wryly. "Just listened from down here."

They sat in silence for a moment, enjoying the peaceful sunrise, drinking their coffee, and not mentioning the ghost.

"Are we going to talk about it?" Annie asked, putting her empty cup on the table.

Swift grunted, shifting on the sofa.

"I'd rather talk about my wife than reminisce about nearly crapping myself because of something that may or may not have been in my bedroom."

"Your wife?" Annie was not expecting that. "Go on then."

She wrapped herself up in the blanket again and sat back, intrigued. The lighter and warmer the room got; the dafter Annie felt about the whole idea of a ghost. Truth was, she never wanted to speak of it again, and with only two nights left at the cottage, Annie figured they could keep the lights on and maybe sleep down here. But Swift's wife was a ghost in her own right. Missing apparently, according to the station gossip.

"It's a long story," said Swift.

"We've got a long time until the village awakens," Annie answered, not wanting him to back out now.

Swift scratched his cheek, looking like a bear with a sore head.

"Okay," he said, softly. "Seeing as it's you. Just don't go talking about this with Rose, and definitely not Tink. Or anyone at the station for that matter."

Rose was Annie's best friend and police station receptionist. She normally told her everything, but for Swift, she'd make an exception.

"Pinky swear," Annie said, holding up her left hand and wiggling her little finger.

"Sophia and I were a couple from a very young age," he started, and Annie was transfixed by the way Swift's eyes glossed over, his jaw set. "We met at school events, her school and mine would share a minibus to sporting events, that kind of thing." From the limited knowledge Annie had of Swift she guessed he was talking about private schools. "We hit it off and started dating. Both of us left school with good qualifications and headed off to separate universities. Sophia to Oxford, me to Exeter, but even though we were miles away from each other we stayed together. Her family is old money, they have all these rules about relationships so when we left uni it was either get married or spilt up."

Swift rubbed at his face again, both palms scraping down his cheeks, rasping against his stubble.

"Did you want to get married?" asked Annie.

He tilted his head and pursed his lips.

"It wasn't that I didn't want to get married," he said. "I just didn't want to get married by anyone else's rules."

Annie gave a small humourless laugh. Swift wasn't one for following rules.

"But I loved Sophia so we made a compromise," he continued. "We got married within a few months of finishing uni, but we did it our way. Eloping to Gretna. Her parents were livid."

He smiled, focusing over Annie's shoulder at the wall behind her but his mind was elsewhere. He sighed, digging the heels of his hands into his eyes.

"What happened to her?" Annie asked, jolting Swift from his daydreams.

"Nothing," he said, sighing again. "Absolutely nothing."

Annie wrinkled her nose. *What?*

"But everyone says…" she started, stopping quickly when she realised he might not know what the rest of the station have to say about Mrs Swift.

Swift's eyebrow shot up.

"I know what everyone says," he replied. "And that's half the reason no-one really knows!"

"You've lost me." She shook her head.

"That's what Sophia said too." Swift burst out laughing, wiping his mouth with the back of his hand. "Look, she left me, okay. One weekend about five years ago, we were supposed to go away together. I'd booked the Monday off which is unheard of for me so obviously the whole team was talking about it. Except, come Friday, Sophia packs a bag and tells me she's moving out and has fallen in love with some git called Kenneth. A bloody farmer. A north Norfolk farmer, to boot. Old money and very rich in land. She said I was holding her back." He threw his hands up in the air.

"The way my parents made their money isn't my fault! And she'd known that, up until I was in high school I wasn't rich, so it was never about the money for me. But as soon as she hit thirty, boom, it was as though she decided to go on the hunt for someone more like her. Can't say I blame her really, I mean, you've stayed at my house, it's not exactly the Ritz."

"Urgh, it's amazing," Annie blurted, thinking of the three turrets and the gothic red brick home.

"Not amazing enough," Swift said, sadly. "She's living on a three-hundred-acre country estate nowadays."

"Some people are never happy, Swift," she said. "It's not your fault. But why do people think she's missing?"

He dropped his head into his hands.

"Because," he said, his voice muffled by his fingers. "When I got back to work on the Tuesday everyone asked me how the weekend away had gone and if Sophia had enjoyed herself. I think they must have thought we were trying to make little Swift babies or something. So, to save face, instead of saying she'd left me, I said *I don't know how Sophia is because I don't know where she is.*

"The story got away from me. But really, a police officer who didn't report a missing wife? That was never going to be me, was it? I've never really spoken about it since the hubbub died down, figured people would stop caring. It's nice to know that every new member of staff is warned that I have a missing wife."

"It wasn't quite like that," Annie said, remembering how Rose had warned her against Swift because he might try to sleep with her. Her cheeks heated.

"I remember." Swift's lips curled into a cheeky smile.

Swift's phone buzzed along the table, the screen flashing.

"Saved by the bell," Annie said, quietly, getting up to make more coffee. She thought they'd need it. Tink was calling.

SEVENTEEN

"Interesting," Swift said, pacing back and forth across the small living room. "Very interesting."

Annie had given up pretending she wasn't listening and given up making more coffee. What Tink was relaying to Swift was obviously far more important than caffeine. He had that steely look about him as he marched between the sofa and the window, skirting around the coffee table that looked as though it would whack him right in the shins with each lap of the room.

Annie was still, her tongue stuck firmly between her front teeth in concentration, but it was no good, she couldn't hear what the DS was saying on the other end of the phone.

"Get those files emailed over to me, asap," Swift said. "And Tink, good work."

He ended the call and spun around on the balls of his feet to face Annie.

"Well?" she asked, drawing out the vowel.

"Nothing on Madeleine Cardeal, she vanished around the early nineties. Tink is still searching. But it seems that some of the people living in Ethlake aren't being totally honest with us." Swift, sucked at his teeth, Annie could practically hear his mind whirring.

"Who? Why?" She had no patience on a good day, but with no sleep her patience was as thin as the walls of a cheap motel.

"Our local friendly bar man?" said Swift, perching on the arm of the sofa. "Lewis? He has a record. Lewis served six months for fraud. Tink is sending over more details. And, get this, even Alf was given a rap on the knuckles for joy riding when he was in his teens."

"Woah." Annie's eyes widened. "Two people in a small village like this? Maybe there's something in the water."

"There's certainly something alright," Swift said. "Can we go and get breakfast at the pub, I'm famished, and I want to speak to Lewis again."

Annie placed a hand on Swift's arm as he stood from the sofa.

"Joe," she said, putting gentle pressure on his forearm. "You said some people here aren't being honest with us?"

"Yeah," he spluttered out a laugh. "No wonder Isla and Lewis want rid of us."

"But Swift," Annie added. "We're not here on a case, we're here to find Mim and have stumbled on something peculiar. So you have to remember that members of the public don't often go around telling strangers that they have a criminal record, do they?"

"Yeah, but." Swift opened his mouth to comeback, and promptly closed it again, his jaw slack.

"You can't suddenly start questioning them about their pasts. No-one knows we're police except the vicar, and I can't imagine she'll be shouting it from the rooftops. If it comes out you're a DI and we're staying in a village of criminals then imagine how people will react then."

Swift laughed.

"Pitchforks at dawn."

"Exactly. So let's calm down a bit and use our disguise to our advantage. Besides, what is it you're hoping to achieve?"

Swift drew his dressing gown around his body, wrapping his arms across his broad chest.

"I'm one hundred percent with you to find out as much as we can about Mim," he said. "But we've hit a brick wall for some reason, and I think everything goes back to the Harpers and the witch. And, though I am ready to pack up the car and leave right now—the idea of spending another night here makes me want to cry—I can't not scratch that itch."

"Me neither," Annie said, shaking her head. "Or me too, I'm too tired to work out which one it is. We've got three days left. Let's make the most of them. Deal?"

"Deal." Swift gave a firm nod. "But O'Malley? Can we go up and get dressed at the same time? I'm too scared to go on my own."

———

THEY STOOD AT THE TOP OF THE HILL, THE CHURCH and the water tower sentinel on either side of them. The early sun beat down on their heads, the sound of the birds lifting their spirits. Down the lane a delivery van was parked outside the pub, a man in blue overalls shifted heavy boxes from the back into the pub garden. As they walked further down the hill the green came into view. It was the start of the school day; parents kissed their children goodbye then went off to whatever would keep them busy until quarter past three. Those children probably wouldn't give a moment's thought to what their mums and dads got up to, they were too young. Annie knew from experience, at that age the world revolved around the children and if there was someone to collect them on time, they were happy not knowing what had happened during the six hours they were away.

As Annie had grown older, she often wondered what happened between her parents during school hours to make the atmosphere so heavy at home. But she never asked. Maybe she should have.

"Do you think the pub is open yet?" Annie asked as they rounded the bottom of the hill, the ducks flapping across the pond.

Her question was answered by the gaggle of the hen party as they stepped out of the pub and into the sunshine, picnic baskets in hand.

"Good morning, fellow ghost hunters," Zoe said, her engagement ring glistening in the sun, though her skin looked lacklustre today. "Up and at the spectres early today?"

Annie raised a hand in greeting.

"Morning," she said, smiling. "Off anywhere nice?"

Zoe raised her wicker basket and lifted off the chequered towel.

"We're going to the next village over today," she said. "Having a day away from the ghosts. They've got a lido and an outdoor cinema so we're setting up there for the day. Bubbles and everything. Lewis made these for us, isn't he lovely?"

Swift cleared his throat and Annie jumped in before he could give away Lewis' secret.

"Enjoy yourselves, won't you?" she said, her stomach rumbling at the sight of sausage rolls and scotch eggs.

"Here," Jessica piped up, lifting her sunglasses onto the top of her head. She looked tired too, and a little green around the gills. Hangover probably, Annie thought. "How did we do the other evening? Did we make good witches?"

"The very best," Swift said, tipping a non-existent hat. "And that's not meant as an insult."

They all giggled and set off on their way for a day of cinema and swimming. Annie wished she could join them; her own holiday was not turning out to be as relaxing as she'd hoped it would be. Though she had been primed for an emotional reunion, she hadn't factored in the hauntings and the missing family.

Swift pushed open the door to the pub and let Annie go first. Lewis was behind the bar, unpacking bottles of lemonade.

"Morning," he said, his smile wide like a crocodile. "Are you after a picnic too? Because you have to order those twenty-four hours in advance."

"Just some breakfast, please," said Swift, leaning on the bar. "If that's up for offer?"

"Find a seat and I'll bring some breakfast menus over," Lewis replied, slamming a bottle down on the bar and immediately lifting it up and checking the base was still intact. "Won't be a minute."

They sat at the back of the room, behind the central beam and hidden away from the bar.

"Do you think it's too early for a glass of wine?" Annie asked, only half joking.

"I need a shot of something after last night," Swift agreed. "But only to chase away the fear."

Lewis appeared by the table, two laminated menus in his hands. He put them down and picked a notebook out of his pocket.

"You wouldn't be the only guests needing alcohol after staying at Crow Cottage." He tapped a pencil on the notepad.

"Really? What do other people say?" Annie asked, curious. "About… you know, the ghosts?"

She could feel her cheeks heating even acknowledging the words.

"Oh, we have had all sorts of rumours over the years," Lewis said, putting the pen behind his ear and pocketing his notepad. He leant a fist on the table, relaxing his hips. "Some people think it's Mrs Harper, some have said it's the witch in child form, a missing girl from the olden days maybe."

"And what do you think?" Swift asked, skirting his eyes down the menu.

"Me?" Lewis asked. "I'm not one to say. Too much respect, here. I don't want to cause trouble."

"Respect for the witch?" asked Annie.

Lewis stood back upright, plucking his pen from behind his ear. A strand of greasy hair flopped away from his head with the movement, bouncing around like a singer's microphone.

"For the witch," he said, nodding, sending the strand of hair haywire. "The curse on the village, for the sacrifices already made. We don't want anyone else to get hurt now, do we?"

His eyes bore into Annie, steely like daggers. Then his persona flipped like a pancake.

"Anyway," he said cheerily. "What can I get you for breakfast?"

EIGHTEEN

Annie and Swift ate their breakfast in silence, the pub growing busier as they tucked into thick sausages and home-made baked beans washed down with builder's tea. Other villagers came and went. Some collecting what looked like home-made lunches, others stopping for a coffee and a chat. With each punter there grew a sense of excitement throughout the bar, like the chatter before a party or a good night out.

Lewis was in his element, greeting them like the old friends they were. Dishing out caffeinated drinks and plans for the upcoming weekend. Annie couldn't help but feel in the way, their eyes often drawn to her and Swift hiding in the corner, their conversations hushed so low she couldn't hear what the villagers were saying.

"No Alf?" An older woman Annie recognised from the village green on the first night. "That's unusual for him this close to Beltane."

She took her tea in a china cup with a saucer. Annie watched as she perched on the bar stool in a two piece with a tweed skirt that made the action difficult.

"He'll be saving his repentance for the ones who matter," Duncan replied from across the bar. "Not practising them on the local barman."

The older woman waved a hand towards Duncan, shooing him the way she might shoo a wasp.

"Away with you Hankinson," she said, drawing her lips into a thin painted line. "Or you'll be next."

"I'm off to see the vicar right after I've finished my bap." Duncan held up his roll, dripping with egg yolk. "I've a lot to get off my chest before tomorrow."

His eyes found Annie across the room as he spoke, quickly looking away, his cheeks heating.

"Why do you think they're all talking of repenting?" Annie whispered, putting down her cutlery.

Swift shook his head, his mouth full. The pub had hushed again, rock music playing quietly over the tinny stereo system did little to alleviate Annie's tension. The atmosphere felt electric, as though if she touched the wall her hair would stand on end.

"I don't know," Swift said, taking a swig of tea. "Maybe they're all worried about Sunday. May the first. Didn't someone say if the village isn't doing as well as it should be then the witch will make her anger known. Or something along those lines?"

"Gerry," Annie answered. "Yeah, he did."

Swift wiped his mouth with the paper napkin, narrowing his eyes. But their attention was drawn by the pub door swinging open and Gerry himself walking in. He glanced around the bar, nodding his head in greeting to Lewis, the old woman, and Duncan. As his eyes fell on Annie and Swift, they lingered, his jaw slackening. One by one the others followed his gaze until they were all staring at the two visitors to the village. The music on the tinny speaker fell quiet as the song ended and Annie felt as though she'd been sucked into a vacuum. She swallowed, trying to pop the bubble from her ears.

"Do you fancy taking one last turn about the village?" Swift said quietly, leaning into Annie. "Before they lynch us where we sit?"

"Yes please," she said, urgently, thinking she'd rather be anywhere than here right now. "I'm still no closer to finding Mim and it's better than sitting here and being whispered about, or going back to the cottage and running into another ghost."

A shudder ran across her neck, and she hugged her arms close to her body as Swift put his cutlery down with a loud clatter.

While Swift paid at the bar, Annie slipped out the back of the pub and through the garden to the lane. The green was empty, but it must be playtime for the little school as the children were out in force in the playground, their shouts and laughter drifting across the grass.

The bonfire stood like a deity at the pinnacle of the green, taller than it was even yesterday. A temporary fence had been erected around its base, bright orange as a warning to stay away. How were they supposed to scare off the hedgehogs with that great hulking thing in the way? The church bell tolled, loud and clear, echoing over the children's laughter. With the blue skies and the heat from the sun, the village green should have been picture perfect against the ringing of the bells. But Annie couldn't help feeling nervous. The bells ringing a warning, the children's screams mounting. A hand touched her shoulder and made her jump.

"That was a little tense," Swift said, removing his hand as though he'd had an electric shock. "Sorry, I didn't mean to make you jump."

"I feel like an actor about to take to the stage," she explained as they started to walk down the lane towards the shop. "Or maybe a condemned man about to walk the mile is a better analogy."

"You feel like something is about to happen, you mean?" Swift asked. "Me too."

Annie nodded, not able to describe the sensation of impending doom without calling it just that. She had the itch at the back of her head that someone was watching them, much like when she'd been in the shower, aware of another presence. She glanced back over her shoulder and her pace quickened.

"Swift," she hissed, drawing her eyebrows together. "Look."

Swift looked behind them, his eyes widening. The children had stopped playing and were standing in a line by the fence, silent as the grave, watching Annie and Swift. And at the door to the pub, spilled out onto the lane were Lewis, Gerry, and Duncan. Just standing. Watching.

Swift locked his arm through Annie's and sped up. They passed by the shop and carried on down the lane, back the way they've driven five days ago when they'd first arrived in Ethlake. It was the first time they've ventured back this way since then and when they passed the bend in the lane that took them out of the village and away from the prying eyes, Annie felt the elastic band around her chest ping free and her ears pop.

"Oh my god." Annie turned to Swift. "Did you feel that?"

The answer was obvious in the way Swift's whole body looked a few stone lighter and his eyes less hooded. He moved his body back and forth, between the invisible veil that hung between Ethlake and the neighbouring village, scratching his hand over his jaw.

"Weird," he said, coming to a standstill. "This whole place is just incredibly weird."

"It's scary," Annie added.

He led them along the lane a little further, to a spot where the hedges thinned giving way to beautiful vistas on both sides. Sweeping hills fell away from the tarmac down to the valleys and the rivers below. The fields were a sparkling yellowy green, like the skin of a Golden Delicious fresh from the tree. A stile cut through a gap in the hedge, a wooden signpost pointed the direction of the public footpath one way, a bridal path the other.

"Shall we?" Swift asked.

Annie paused to roll up the sleeves of her jumper, before taking the footpath that curled up the hill and back towards the church.

"That group of hens," Annie said, taking care to walk down the side of the field without turning her ankle again.

"The ones that are clucking like deranged raptors every morning?" Swift asked, bounding up next to her, treading between the short crops.

"What?"

"What?"

"I mean the women, the hen party," Annie said, feeling a smile creep onto her face. "Not real hens."

"Oh," Swift laughed. "Then yes, I do know that group of hens. Just as loud but much less annoying than the feathered version. What about them?"

"Why are they being given the VIP treatment, yet everyone is muttering about us behind our backs?"

Swift dropped back behind Annie as the crops grew too high to step between.

"Maybe because they're being good tourists?" Swift replied. "Actually *hunting* ghosts. Not asking questions about missing sisters. Not police."

Annie pondered his reply as she traversed around a knoll of trees cutting into the field. The view when she'd passed them was breath-taking. The rise and fall of the hills looked like an oil painting where the light caught the grass. From where she was standing, Annie could see all the way down into the valley to Alf's farmhouse. She could see him, a small figure standing among his cars. There was someone with him, and from the way she was dressed, Annie could tell it was the vicar.

"I wonder if there's something going on between them?" Annie asked Swift as they fell side by side again and set off towards the church. "Can vicars have relationships? Is that allowed?"

'I think so," Swift said. "But I'm getting my knowledge here from my memory of the Vicar of Dibley."

A laugh bubbled out of Annie; it was a welcome distraction from all the tension she'd been carrying.

"Though I think," Swift continued. "That it's more likely she's helping him repent his misspent youth."

"What?"

"The cars," Swift added, prompting Annie's brain to catch up.

"Oh yeah," she said, looking at the yard full. "Hopefully he paid for these ones though. And wasn't that when he was a teen? How long must one repent for, for it to work?"

"Asking for a friend, there, O'Malley?"

"Oy." Annie hit Swift gently on the arm, trotting away from him across the field. He made to chase after her.

Squealing, Annie started running, trying to stay upright as Swift followed. She was laughing so much it was proving hard. Swift was fast and wearing sensible shoes. She ducked under his arm and doubled back on her footsteps, but it was futile. He caught her, grabbing her around the waist from behind and swinging her around in a circle. Her eyes streamed with happy tears and as he put her back on the ground she doubled over, hands on her knees to stop herself from collapsing onto the furrows of earth.

"You're out of order, Swift," she choked through bouts of laughter. "I've got nothing to repent for."

Swift brushed his hands together, his cheeks pink with exertion.

"No?" he asked, his eyes darkening as he looked her way.

Annie straightened up and cleared her throat, her pulse pounding in her neck. She could feel her own cheeks redden.

"Nothing quite as bad as pretending to have a missing wife to avoid looking like a knob, no," she said, spinning around and marching back towards the church, hurt grin making her cheeks hurt.

"Oof," Swift shouted after her. "Low blow, O'Malley. Low blow."

Annie swung her arms as she walked, her body felt ten times lighter. And as she threw her head over her shoulder to check Swift wasn't really annoyed with her, she caught sight of Alf and the vicar again. Only this time they were both looking up the hill right back at her, their arms raised in a wave, their faces open with smiles. Annie waved back, feeling Swift's hand on her elbow.

"How about we get back to the cottage, get in the car, and get out of Ethlake for the rest of the day?" he said, slipping his arm through hers again.

"Deal."

"Deal."

They walked up past the church and back to the lane, all the while Annie could feel the eyes of Alf and the vicar burning though the back of her head.

NINETEEN

SATURDAY

Annie was awoken the next morning by a stream of expletives from the neighbouring sofa. She ran a hand though her hair, tugging out the knots and dragging it up into a bun. Looking at her watch, she was surprised to see it was almost eleven. She sat up, hugging the duvet close to her. Swift was hidden under his pillow, his hands holding it around his face. Now his swear words were muffled, Annie could hear the gentle rasp of the chickens outside.

"You'll suffocate," she said, sliding off the sofa and going to put the kettle on.

Swift gave a one-word answer and held on tighter. He was right, the chickens were being very noisy this morning, their low rumble of clucking reaching a crescendo of a squawk that made it sound as though they were being slaughtered. She pushed the window open in the kitchen and shooed them away.

Annie and Swift had gone to the neighbouring town yesterday afternoon, and not come back until it was dark, and they could sneak into the cottage unnoticed. A trip around some local shops and a meal in a restaurant had brightened Annie's day no end. It had been good to get away from the suffocating blanket of Ethlake. No longer did it feel like a welcome break, an idyll; it was more like a prison with invisible bars. They'd opted for the sofas because neither of them wanted to be on their own, despite not mentioning the ghost again.

No wonder Mim isn't here anymore, Annie thought, sadly, as she poured boiling water over two teabags.

She took the drinks back through and left Swift's on the coffee table while she went upstairs to go and get washed and dressed. The cottage was warm, soaking up the sun's rays and clinging on to them with its thick walls and wool-lined attic. As she rounded the top of the stairs, the spring in her step unwound a little. Her bedroom door was ajar, but Annie could have sworn she'd clicked it shut last night after gathering up her duvet and pillow. Any rooms they weren't using they'd decided to keep closed, in case they had another night visitor, at least that way the singing and the glow could be blocked out. Swift's door was wide on its hinges too. His little bedroom on view from the top of the stairs. She stuck her head in, noted the neatly packed case on the floor, and the side table with his book, water, and his wallet all at right angles. But his wallet was open, catching her eye as it had moved a fraction out of line. The metal of the police badge reflected the sun from the window, glaring into her eyes as she went in the room and walked towards it.

Inside, the temperature had dropped a few degrees. Annie frowned, flipping the wallet closed, and taking in the room in more detail. The window was shut and there was no way Swift would have left his wallet open on his police badge. Not even if he'd been chased out of here by the ghost itself. It went against all his instincts. But it didn't look as though anything else in the room was out of place. Even his used towel was folded neatly next to the cupboard door, ready to be taken to the laundry.

She exited, pulling his door shut behind her and feeling the latch click under her fingers. Her own room was less tidy, but that was her own mess, not that of a ghost. A quick look allayed her fears that something else would be missing or out of place. The hairbrush, Swift's wallet, his razor, the doll. A cold draft wrapped around her bare ankles from the landing, making her shiver.

What's that? Stepping into her room, Annie shut the door and blocked out the draft.

Turning on the shower, Annie pottered about in her room while the water warmed up. She plugged in her phone to charge and remade her bed, whistling to herself to stave off the quiet. A billow of steam puffed out from under the en-suite door, Annie grabbed her own towels from the floor and headed through. What she saw made her blood run cold.

GET OUT.

Written on the mirror in the condensation.

Two words that stoked fear deep in Annie's stomach.

"Swift," she shouted, stepping backwards into her bedroom. "SWIFT."

The steam followed her out onto the landing, swirling around her knees, blowing towards her by the breeze still coming from Swift's room. She heard his thumping footsteps run up the stairs.

"What is it?" he yelled, his hair all over the place, his t-shirt on back to front. "What's happened."

"My mirror." Annie lifted a hand and pointed at her open bedroom door.

Swift dashed into Annie's room, leaving her alone on the landing with the mist and her thoughts. They tumbled together; one as chaotic as the other. The cottage was haunted, there really was no question about that. Not after everything that had happened. The figure from the shower. Items moved or missing. The singing. The girl she'd seen in Swift's bedroom. And now this. But what was the ghost warning them about? Why did it want them to leave?

Moments later, Swift stumbled out of her room, a tangle of clothes in his arms.

"Put these on in my room and let's get out of here." He handed Annie the clothes and guided her through to his bedroom. "I'll face the door. Hurry."

The selection of clothes Swift had picked from the pile on Annie's floor were a mixture. A pair of jeans with a striped t-shirt and a knitted sweater which Annie was thankful for. The lacy purple bra and matching knickers, less so. Packed only on the off chance of a night out, Annie was usually in wash grey granny pants and a vest top. She blushed bright red as she pulled them on, glad Swift was facing the door, and glad of the cool breeze still circulating around his room.

"Done," she said, buttoning the flies on her jeans. "Your turn."

She spun around, surprised to see Swift already dressed and running his hands through his hair to try and tame the nest.

"Pack your stuff," he said, walking over to his suitcase and folding the clothes he'd worn overnight. He patted them down on the top and pulled the lid closed.

"What? No." Annie blurted. "It's just one more night. Please. The ghost may not want us here, but I need to try one last time to find out more about Mim."

Swift straightened up. His face was pale, shocking purple rings lined his eyes. Annie dropped her guard, more than once had her instinct gotten the job done but not before getting them in trouble. These last couple of years she'd thought Swift was the outlier, the one who would push back against the rules to get answers. But maybe it was her. Maybe that's why he was so adamant to get her on the team. Did this make her a maverick?

"Annie," Swift said, placing a hot hand on her sleeve. "I don't think we're safe here."

"But what if Mim wasn't safe here either?" She felt the wind drop from her sails. "What if something happened to her here in Ethlake and that's why everyone is lying to me? One last chance. Please, Swift. Please."

He searched her face, stripping her of any barrier she'd placed between them. Eventually, he shut his eyes and blew out a thin stream of air.

"You're worse than I am, O'Malley," he said, holding his hands up. "Okay. Okay, one more night. But let's get out of here because this place is giving me the creeps."

They took the stairs as quickly as possible, slipping their feet into their shoes by the door and stepping out into the warm sunshine. Annie popped a couple of bits of chewing gum, running her tongue over her fuzzy teeth. She hated not brushing them, but she hated ghosts more.

"Who've we got, then?" Swift asked as they walked down the hill to the village. "Isla in the shop was definitely not telling the truth about Mim when you asked."

"And her son, Duncan, practically told me he knew Mim," Annie added. "He warned me off asking about her."

"Yep," agreed Swift. "Then there was Lewis, he is a worse liar than you."

"And the vicar?" Annie asked, ignoring the jibe. "She isn't allowed to lie outright, surely? Maybe she's our best bet?"

The church loomed over them as they spoke. Rising out of the earth with the sun behind it, the stonework fell into the shadows. The windows like black holes.

"Can we go to the shop first?" Swift asked. "I need something to eat."

Relief flooded Annie. For reasons she couldn't put her finger on, she wasn't quite ready to go to the church again either.

They continued down the hill, stepping out of the shadows of the church and the water tower into bright sunshine once again. The grass of the green looked thick and luscious. The pond water sparkled in the light. Even the ducks were resting on the banks, their eyes closed, basking in the warmth. But Annie couldn't shift the icy feeling that had burrowed into her bones and settled there like damp.

It felt as though the village was coming to life. People were heading to the green, the front doors of the houses that surrounded the centre of the village were propped open, and happy faces greeted each other. The shop and pub were welcoming too, their signs out and their own entrances wide open. Annie raised a hand to wave at the older woman who'd been in the pub yesterday morning as she leant against her door-frame, cup in hand, talking to a neighbour. The woman looked right through Annie, going back to her conversation as though Annie wasn't even there.

"Rude," Annie muttered.

"What?" Swift said, turning his attention from the ducks to Annie.

"Nothing," she replied. "I think I'm just hangry."

"Come on then," he said, ducking through the door to the shop. "Breakfast bars on me."

Annie chuckled and followed Swift into the little shop. She perused the aisles, trying to find something that wasn't chocolate or crisps for breakfast and settled on a Rice Crispy Square and a plastic cup of cold Starbucks. Isla was at the till point, the daily paper spread out over the counter.

"Lovely morning," Annie said, hovering next to the counter, not sure where to put her things. "Are you all set for the celebrations tomorrow?"

Isla didn't look up from the gossip pages. Annie scanned the shop for Swift, but he was busy in the small fresh produce section, so she pressed on.

"I know you said you didn't know my sister, Mim," she continued, aware that Isla hadn't even acknowledged she was there. "But she stayed here, and I don't believe someone living in the village wouldn't come into the local shop."

A flicker of something flashed across Isla's face, but she soon rearranged it back to blank. Turning the page of her newspaper, Isla barely even blinked when Swift appeared at the counter, arms laden with fruit and bottled water. Annie looked down at her coffee and biscuit and added it to Swift's burdened arms with a shrug.

"Just these, please, Isla," he said, having the same difficulty as Annie had with the counter covered in newspaper.

Isla didn't move. She didn't look up. Swift and Annie exchanged a look.

"We can't leave without paying," Swift said, shuffling the food onto one arm to reach his wallet in his pocket. An apple fell and rolled across the shop floor, disappearing under the magazine rack.

Annie took Swift's wallet, remembering how it had been laid out on his bedside table that morning. Pulling out a tenner, she left it on top of the article Isla was reading and stormed out of the shop, Swift close behind her.

"There was no way a tenner would cover all this," Swift said, trying to hold an orange with his chin as he juggled the rest of his breakfast.

"She shouldn't have been so rude then, should she." Annie grabbed as much of the fruit as she could, along with her own breakfast. Leaving Swift with the bottled water. "Why did she ignore us?"

Swift shrugged, twisting open one of the bottles and taking a long pull of water.

"Ah, that's so good," he said, offering it to Annie.

She shook her head, poking the straw from her coffee through the lid and sucking. It was cold, and sweet, and caffeinated, just what she needed.

A young teen cycled towards them on a BMX, head forwards, shoulders braced, eyes boring into Annie. He lifted the front wheel up with a jerking motion, balancing in a wheelie inches away from Annie's head. Swift grabbed Annie's arm and pulled her off the road onto the green.

"Watch where you're going," he yelled, water spilling over the top of the bottle as he waved an angry arm.

A thought flashed into Annie's head, so absurd it made her stop in her tracks. The old woman ignored her, Isla couldn't see them, the young boy nearly ran her down with his wheels.

"Oh God, Swift," Annie blurted. "Are we dead? Can they not see us because we're the ghosts?"

TWENTY

Swift looked at Annie as though she was losing the plot. And maybe she was. Lack of sleep was getting to her, and from the pallor of Swift's skin, she'd say it was getting to him too.

"This isn't Sixth Sense, O'Malley," Swift said. "We're not waiting to leave this mortal coil and only hanging on to solve your sister's disappearance."

"Then why is everyone treating us like we're not here?" She flapped her free arm around, indicating the whole of the village green.

"I don't know," Swift said, softly, looking around at the busying grass. "But it's not because we were killed in our sleep by an angry ghost."

He looked at her, a smile creeping onto his face.

He was right. Of course he was right. Looking around the green, the villagers pottered about without a care in the world. Even the four women away on their hen do were helping Gerry string bunting across the trees at the far end of the common. Their dresses blew in the breeze, daisy chains sat prettily in crowns around their heads. Annie felt like she and Swift had a comic grey cloud above their heads, perpetually pouring raining on them. Further up the green a group of young men were shifting the barriers away from the bonfire, Duncan among them. Annie started walking in their direction, ignoring the thumping in her chest and the tightness it brought with it.

With the barriers away from the heaving construction, two men brought over a ladder and propped it up against the wooden crates. And while the others got on with scaring away any animals who'd taken residence in the prepped fire, Duncan started to climb the ladder. He was slow and steady, well-practised, Annie thought, because it looked treacherous. Old floorboards stuck out like accusatory fingers; nails still intact. Dismantled wardrobes with screws pointing skywards. Even the wood that had been hacked into smaller pieces for kindling rose into the air like daggers. If Duncan mis stepped, he could slip and fall on any one of them, skewering himself.

Swift stood quietly beside Annie as they watched another young man hand Duncan a long pole. It was much like a jousting pole, though pointed at both ends. Scary enough to make any lingering hedgehogs run for cover. But Duncan wasn't using it to scare away the wildlife. He found the centre of the bonfire from the top and rammed the pole into it as hard as he could. Annie placed a trembling hand against her lips, stepping backwards away from the bonfire. It wasn't a pole; it was a stake. And Duncan was preparing it for tomorrow, strapping it up with rope ready for what-ever they had planned to burn.

Swift took a step back, coming into line with Annie.

"Maybe they're not ignoring us because we're already dead," he whispered, his voice shaking. "Maybe it's because we're about to be burned at the stake."

Annie flung her head towards him, searching Swift's face for any signs of humour, but there was none to be found. Behind them, raised voices carried across the grass. Annie turned to look at where they were coming from. It was Isla and Lewis, squaring off in front of the shop, Isla's arms waving wildly in Annie and Swift's direction while Lewis grew redder by the second. Annie couldn't work out what they were saying, but it was obviously about her and Swift. As Isla raised her hand to strike Lewis' face, the vicar appeared in the shop doorway and grabbed her wrist before she made contact. The two proprietors looked ashamed; their heads dropped in embarrassment. The vicar gathered them into her fold, and before long they slunk back to their work and the old woman started on up the hill towards the church.

"Go and talk to Duncan," Annie said to Swift, thinking quickly. "See what you can find out about this whole *burning at the stake* thing."

"Guv," Swift said, saluting Annie. "Where are you going?"

"To find out about Mim once and for all." She set off over the grass towards the pond, trying to cut the vicar off before she reached the church and locked the door behind her.

"Vicar," Annie shouted as she came in earshot.

The vicar didn't stop, she didn't even turn around. This wasn't fair. Surely a woman of the cloth wouldn't be permitted to ostracise someone in need of help.

"Vicar, please?" she shouted louder. "Stop."

The old woman bowed her head and came to a stop in front of the entrance to the graveyard. Annie jogged a little to catch up with her.

"Thank you," she puffed. "I was beginning to think I was invisible."

The vicar looked around, scanning both up the hill and down, then ushered Annie towards her with twisted fingers.

"Come inside, quickly," she whispered, hobbling towards the church.

Annie followed her inside silently and watched as the vicar pushed the door shut behind them, drawing a large metal bolt across, trapping them both. The silence was absolute. The kind of silence that could have come from inside her head. Using her therapist's instinct, Annie looked around for another way out. A quick escape. The pews lined on either side all the way down to the pulpit. Behind the stage was a curtain, and she'd put money on that leading to the small entrance at the side of the church. Annie's skin was prickled with goosebumps as the old woman came towards her, knuckled fingers outstretched.

"Calm yourself, dear," she said, putting her hand on Annie's arm. It was like ice. "I'm not going to hurt you."

The vicar's words did little to allay Annie's fears, the coldness reaching all the way from her hands to her eyes.

"Sit." It wasn't a question.

Annie took a seat at the edge of the pew, the vicar sitting over the aisle. The woman rested an arm against the wood and darted her tongue across her dry lips.

"I didn't get the chance to speak to you before," Annie started, trying not to let this woman get to her. "But

I'm here looking for my sister. Mim. Do you know her?"

The vicar looked up to the carved ceiling, her lips moving quickly but silently. Outside a large crow swept passed the stained windows, a dark shadow cutting through the scenes of Jesus on his cross. It cawed loudly and soared towards the sun.

"People are scared." It was as though vicar hadn't heard Annie speak. "This village is bound by age old beliefs that have been passed down from parent to child. When outsiders come here asking too many questions the villagers get troubled."

"But I'm just trying to find my sister," Annie cried. "We've only been asking more questions because of all the weird things that have happened. People denied knowing her, yet I *know* she was here. I've seen her name in the census. Yes, this place may be haunted by a family who went missing ages ago, but at the moment all I care about is finding Mim."

The vicar tapped her fingers on her knee, her knuckles thick and round, her nails yellowing with age.

"The village almost lost everything back in the eighties," she went on, her throat rasping. "It's prosperous now, thriving. They don't want to lose it all again. And it wasn't you I was referring to when I said too many questions were being asked. It was Mim."

The temperature in the church dropped below zero. Annie couldn't control the clashing of her teeth or the thickness in her throat.

"She was here." Annie could barely breathe. "What happened to her?"

The vicar's eyes swept across the church to the far end. Annie heard the clatter of a door and saw the vicar's translucent skin pale even further.

"I haven't told anyone you're police." The vicar peeled a bottle from under her cassock and took a long drink, clear liquid dribbling down the sides of her mouth and getting caught in the ruts of skin. "But you should know that if they find out, you're in danger. Anyone who tips the balance is in danger. It's what I told Mim. She was as nosey as you are."

Amongst the fear, Annie felt a rush of pride for her younger sister.

"What happened to her?" Annie asked again, losing patience. "Did you all hurt her? Where is she?"

"I have never hurt anyone," the vicar rasped, her eyes narrow. "So help me God. I may have done some terrible things in my life, but I have never hurt anyone."

Annie's blood ran cold.

"But I'm not the village," the vicar continued. Her moment of aggression seemed to sap her last ounce of strength. "Mim was in danger. I helped her leave. She did get out in time. But I don't know where she went, we thought it safer that way."

"Safer for who?" Annie shouted back, pushing herself to her feet. "You say you never hurt anyone, but staying silent when those around you do hurt people, is just as bad."

The curtain moved, catching Annie's eye. She ran for the door, hefting the metal lock in her hands and trying to drag it open. The vicar got to her feet, pushing herself up with a wobble, she started towards Annie. The lock wouldn't budge, Annie couldn't get out. The vicar was getting closer, and Annie pushed harder at the bolt. The curtain started to draw back.

"Come on," she yelled. "Come on."

The old woman gave a low blood-curdling cry.

"Ruuuuuun," she called, only feet away from where Annie was struggling with the door.

Then, as she reached out a hand to grab Annie's sleeve, the bolt slipped through the casing, the door swung towards Annie, hitting her painfully in the shoulder. And she ran. Out of the church, past the gravestones, and down the lane to the green. She kept running, sweeping her gaze across the field to try and find Swift.

As her feet pounded along the tarmac, she saw Gerry and the school children practicing around the May Pole. Their faces covered by their handmade masks. The splash of colour, the crass way the masks depicted the sacred bull, the idea that absolutely anyone could be hiding amongst them as they darted around chaotically, made Annie's eyes stream. Though the celebrations weren't until tomorrow, the crowds were growing, making it hard to spot Swift among the people. But she caught sight of him deep in conversation with Duncan at the edge of the woods. Glancing behind her to make sure she wasn't being chased, Annie cut across the green speeding up towards her boss.

He must have sensed her coming, turning his head in her direction, and holding his hand up to stop her from taking them both off their feet.

"O'Malley," he said, grabbing her shoulders. "What's gotten into you?"

She took a breath, looking between the young man and Swift. Duncan looked at her with the confident reproach afforded to those on the crest of adolescence; Annie wasn't sure if she could trust him. Battening down the fear instead, she tried to tell Swift what had happened by telekinesis alone. Her eyes searching his. Wanting to tell him that Mim had lived here, that she'd been in danger. Hell, Duncan had probably known her.

"Just couldn't find you, that's all." she tried to smile, feeling droplets of sweat trickle down her temple. "Duncan, nice to see you."

She studied him closely, could he tell she was scared? Did he know she knew about Mim?

"Duncan here was just telling me about the bonfire," Swift said, letting go of her shoulders after giving her a gentle squeeze. "How they attach a sacrificial beast to the stake to show the witch they're on her side."

Annie's stomach lurched.

"What kind of beast?" she asked, irritation rising in her at the smirk on Duncan's face.

"We don't know until tomorrow." He shrugged, swallowing, and scratching the back of his neck. "It's all part of the ceremony. The adults draw names out of a bag." His face paled as he spoke, the youthful demeanour long gone. "Anyway, I've got stuff to be getting on with. See ya."

He ducked his head down and disappeared into the crowds. Swift rubbed Annie's arm, concern on his face.

"You really okay?" he asked.

"No," she said. "Let's walk."

She led them into the woods where the noise of the crowd and the heat of the afternoon sun fell away.

There, in the quiet, away from prying eyes, Annie told Swift what she'd learnt from the vicar. How Mim had been in Ethlake and how the villagers had chased her away. How someone else had been in the church with them and scared Annie away before she could find out anymore.

"And she had no idea where Mim went?" Swift asked, as he paced over the moss underfoot, flattening it down until it was as brown as the earth. "She didn't say which of the villagers had been threatening?"

Annie remembered the way the vicar had looked as she'd fumbled with the door.

"I think it was the whole damn village," she said, shuddering. "This place is poison."

Something itched away at the back of Annie's brain, she could feel the beginnings of the answers moulding themselves around her synapses. And then, in the feint thrum of chirping insects and rustling leaves, Annie heard something that made her heart stop.

TWENTY-ONE

"You hear that?" she whispered, grabbing Swift's arm, cocking her head to hear over the sound of her own blood.

Swift squeezed his eyes shut and they stood among the trees and listened. There, a child singing. No, not just a child, a whole school of them.

Beannaich, a Thrianailt fhioir nach gann,
Mi fein, mo cheile agus mo chlann,
Mo chlann mhaoth's am mathair chaomh 'n an ceann,
Air chlar chubhr nan raon, air airidh chaon nam beann,
Air chlar chubhr nan raon, air airidh chaon nam beann.

Their voices were so gentle, Annie wasn't sure they were real. But as the song swelled to a crescendo, Swift's eyes flew open, and she knew he could hear it too.

"The ghost?" he hissed, dropping his head near to Annie's cheek.

The little kernels of information tumbled into place. The doll being moved, the young ghost, the writing on her mirror, the stake on the bonfire and Duncan's fear as he spoke of the parents' choice of what to burn. She couldn't verbalise her thoughts, not yet, they were still too far away from reach, like a dream she was trying to remember. Turning on her heels, Annie sped back through the woods to the edge of the village green, Swift close on her tail.

It was busy now, full of happy, smiling people dancing with each other. The kind of folk dancing Annie hated at school as it meant partnering up with a boy and swinging each other around by the crooks of their elbows. She pushed through the throngs to the top of the green, following the singing and the chatter of excited children, stopping where they were all gathered at the May Pole. A woman span around and around, her hands above her head, her eyes closed to the sun above her, knocking against Annie as she twisted. It was the teacher, Annie recognised her from the church, and the school playground. Grabbing her shoulder Annie shook her out of her daydream.

"Excuse me," she said, breathlessly. "Excuse me, what are the children doing?"

There were fifteen or so of them, all under ten, girls and boys. They ran around the May Pole, holding imaginary ribbons, ducking in and out of each other's arms as they sang and laughed. The words of the song entrenched in their memories and sang with confidence. The teacher's smiled dropped as she saw who had interrupted her, glancing around as though she'd been caught out, Annie saw fear flash through her eyes.

"They're practising," she said, drawing her smile back as big and as bright as before, like a doll. "For tomorrow's celebration."

Her eyes were fixed on something over Annie's shoulder. Glancing behind her, Annie caught the back of Lewis's head as he disappeared into the crowd.

"Practising?" Annie prompted, her attention back on the teacher.

"Yes," the teacher replied letting out a long breath, her shoulders slumped forwards. "And a little audition of sorts."

Annie's head was swimming, she couldn't hear past the song and the laughter. She moves closer to the teacher as she spoke.

"Audition?"

"Though, of course, all the children get a go on the May Pole," the teacher went on, her body starting to sway softly in dance. "There are a select few who will actually wind the ribbon."

Annie stumbled backwards, treading on Swift's toes. She needed to get out of the crowds. She needed air. Once again, she ran.

Pushing past a family holding hands and skipping around in a circle, Annie burst out of the green and onto the little lane. She ran up the hill, past the shop, past the church and the water tower. She ran all the way across the weed covered gravel driveway of Crow Cottage and unlocked the door with trembling fingers.

"Annie," Swift huffed, drawing breath. "What's wrong? Why did you run? Do you know what's happening here? Talk to me"

He fell in through the doorway after her, kicking off his shoes and flopping down on the sofa. Checking the lane was clear, Annie shut the door and turned the key in the lock.

"I have an idea," she said, sliding the bolt across into its keep.

As darkness fell across the Dales, creeping in through the cottage windows with long, bony fingers, Annie paced around the living room like a caged lion.

"It's nearly time," Swift said, checking his watch and finishing off his tea and toast. "We should head to bed."

Her chest tightened. This was it. She gave a brisk nod and, not breaking stride, headed to the stairs and up into her bedroom. They gave an unspoken acknowledgment to each other at their doors and pushed them closed. Inside her small bedroom, Annie couldn't stop her pacing. It was the only thing barring her mind from racing away with her fears, causing her to run screaming from the cottage. She grabbed her bedside glass and ran clean water in it from the shower room, eyes turned away from the mirror.

Dusk turned to darkness, and soon the owls and the bats were awake, screeching into the night, swooping and soaring through the sky. Pulling the curtains shut, Annie turned off her night light and sat on the edge of her bed, still fully clothed.

It had been there all along, right in front of them, dangled like a carrot. Mim had realised too, and that's why they had chased her away from the village. But what would they have done to her if she hadn't escaped? How determined were the villagers to keep their secrets? There was only one way for Annie to find out if what she believed was true, and it was going to take all her courage to sit tight.

As the hours passed, Annie's eyes grew heavy. Her lids dropped and she felt her head snap up, her heart pounding. And then there it was again, just the same as earlier on the green and two nights ago in this very cottage. Singing. A singular, beautiful voice, pure and chilling. Annie pursed her lips and blew out a breath, standing as quietly as she could from her bed. Creeping across the floor, avoiding the boards that creaked and groaned under her weight, she slid open her door and stepped out onto the landing. The singing grew louder, a faint blue glow passing under Swift's door. She hoped he'd managed to stay awake too, or his frightened awakening burst might ruin Annie's plan.

Standing at Swift's closed door, Annie held her breath, waiting. Then the watch on her wrist vibrated and she tensed, ready for action. Pushing open the bedroom door, Annie flicked on the light switch and saw Swift running across the room towards the airing cupboard. Between them, a young girl, no older than ten, stared at her with wide eyes and a painted face.

"It's okay," Annie said, softly. "We're not going to hurt you."

The girl looked closed to tears, her lip wobbled, her face bright pink through the creamy paint still glowing under the black light held in her shaking hands. She

217

stepped back as Annie tried to coax her to sit down, turning like a mouse and darting towards the cupboard. The girl ran straight into Swift and gave a cry, collapsing to the floor in fear.

"It's okay," Annie said again as the girl curled in on herself on the floorboards.

Swift patted the girl on the head like she was a wild animal and stepped around her to give her more space.

"You're right," he said to Annie, who was looking at him with disbelief. "That water tank is obsolete, which I should have realised given the combi-boiler downstairs. It's an empty shell with stairs behind it."

"I thought so," Annie said, squatting down to the girl and placing a hand on her back. She could feel the rapid rise and fall of her breathing, the hammering of her heart through her ribs. There was nothing to the girl, she was so slight Annie felt as though if she pressed too hard, she'd break her. "Is it all the children? Or just a select few? How did you get picked to come and see us tonight?"

The girl hitched a breath, sniffing loudly under her arms.

"I won," she said, so quietly Annie had to lean in to hear her. "My singing was the best."

"Well I can see why," Annie replied, dropping to her bottom and crossing her legs in front of her. The little girl poked her head out from under an arm, just enough that Annie could see her face luminescent with the black-light and the neon paint designed to emit a ghostly glow. "Your singing was beautiful, and very, very scary."

"Was it?" The girl sniffed.

"The scariest we've heard all week," Annie replied, handing the girl a tissue. "Wasn't it Joe?"

"Terrifying," he said, hovering near the door.

"Look." Annie gestured to Swift. "Swift is a senior detective and he's still scared."

It wasn't a lie either. Swift looked as uncomfortable as Annie had even seen him.

The girl peeked out a little further to look at Swift, a small smile creeping onto her face. She tucked her lips into her mouth.

"What is the song you sing?" Annie asked.

"A blessing for Beltane," the girl whispered, her eyes still on Swift. "If we sing it really well our school will get lots of money."

"Well I think your school is going to be rich, then." Annie smiled and the girl beamed back.

"Really?" She shuffled upright, tucking her hands into the sleeves of her long white dress. "My teacher said we might all be able to get an iPad next year if we do well. Will I get an iPad?"

"I think you will," Annie replied, crossing her fingers behind her back. "You'd best be off, now, so they don't send out a search party. Who is waiting for you out there?"

"Miss Crosby," the girl said, looking down at her hidden hands. "And Mrs Hankinson."

"Where do your parents think you are?" Swift asked from the doorway.

"All of the children have to do it," the girl said, wide-eyed. "Our parents must never know. Please don't tell them."

Annie held her hands up. "We promise not to say a word," she said, smiling. "Now, off you pop. Wipe your tears on the way out."

The girl jumped to her feet and scuttled towards the cupboard, pulling back the cover of the water tank she ran down the stairs, singing as she went.

Swift sat down hard on his bed, running his hands through his hair.

"You were right," he said, as Annie sat next to him.

'Of course I was," she grinned. "When I saw the children dancing and singing earlier, I have to say my first thoughts fell to them being the lambs on the stake."

220

Swift coughed out a laugh, his leg pushing against hers. She could feel the heat of his skin through their clothes.

"But," she went on. "If a child from the village was being sacrificed every year, then that would be a huge news story, not just an urban legend."

"So you think the witch is an urban legend too?" Swift asked, flopping back so his head and shoulders rested on the wall.

"I don't know," Annie said. "This village thrives on its rumours, it's a tourist attraction for good reason, and that brings in an income for everyone here. I think Lewis and Isla are behind it, long term residents working with the school to make sure they're never in the same position they were back in the eighties."

"Yeah," Swift agreed. "Those sounded like hard times. I can sense a *but* coming."

"*But* there is still a missing family at the heart of this village. And I want to know what happened to them."

TWENTY-TWO

SUNDAY

Annie put the last of their bags into the car and slammed shut the boot.

"I think I know what has been bothering me about the cottage," she said to Swift as they gave the rooms one last sweep for belongings.

"Apart from the moving objects, the ghost, the writing on the mirror and the missing family belongings stashed in the cellar, you mean?" He laughed and pulled the cottage door shut, locking it, and sliding the key through the letter box as requested.

Annie batted him on the arm and set off down the hill towards the village green. It was ten and the celebrations had been loud enough to hear from the cottage for at least a couple of hours. Music blared from speakers, and the crowds gathered in force.

"With a staircase to that bloody lean-to, anyone could have come and gone as they pleased." Annie said, stopping at the gate to the graveyard, thrown into shade by the water tower and the church itself. "My hairbrush, your razor; moved by Isla or Lewis while we were out. I think I stumbled upon one of them after I fell in the pond and had to go back and get changed. I think the writing was designed to scare us away because we were asking too many questions."

She set off again, steeling herself for how the villagers would treat them today.

"So what was bothering you, then?" Swift asked.

"The stuff in the cellar." Annie saw the children milling around the May Pole, recognising the little girl who they'd caught last night among them. "It was too clean, too fresh to belong to the missing family."

"You think it was planted there?" asked Swift as he headed straight to a small van advertising coffee.

"I think the whole thing was a farce," she said, as they joined the queue. "A front. They play up to the fears of people who come and stay. Take them for tours of the witch's house, the shrine, scare them half to death in a cottage that is staged as much as a Christmas panto."

"But Gerry's fear was real," Swift said, ordering a flat white and a latte. "He thinks the witch is real."

Annie thanked the barista for her coffee and stepped out of the way.

"So it's just some of the village, then" she said. "The ones who started the rumours. They keep the rest of them on their toes?"

She could feel eyes on her. She knew people were watching what she and Swift were doing. The glances were less subtle now, the whispers louder.

"And we know who started the rumours, don't we?" Swift asked.

"Isla and Lewis." Annie answered.

"You think they had something to do with the Harpers going missing?" Swift said, stepping around a family setting up camping chairs near the May Pole.

"I don't know," Annie said, the hairs on her neck standing to attention as the vicar came into view through the crowds.

The old woman stood at the entrance to the graveyard sipping water from her bottle with one hand, the other tucked into her cassock. She caught sight of Annie, her face froze, her hand midway to her mouth. As quickly as she could the vicar walked down the lane towards them, Annie felt her chest tighten and moved closer to Swift.

"Morning vicar," Swift said, jovially, squeezing Annie's hand.

"You need to go." Her voice was shaking as much as her hands were now. "Leave. I thought I'd made myself clear."

The vicar took a step towards Annie, so close Annie could see the fine specks of powder sitting on the top of her wrinkled skin, the red raw edges of her watery eyes. She smelt like sweat and cheap perfume. Annie felt something move near the top of her leg and jumped away.

"When we first arrived in the church," Annie said, realisation hitting her. "You said '*I wondered when you'd come*', didn't you?"

The vicar nodded, sadly.

"You weren't talking about coming to see you as ghost hunters going to visit the local church, you knew we were police." Annie stopped to take a breath. "You know something, don't you? You thought we'd come *for you*."

"You need to leave." The vicar looked at Annie, not really seeing her, as Alf came up behind her and took her arm. "Or you'll end up just like them."

"Alright, vicar," he said, taking her arm, winking at Annie. "Can I borrow you for a moment?"

As he guided the old woman away, he lifted a bottle of water from his bag, offering it up to her. And the final pieces of the puzzle clicked into place in Annie's head.

"Oh my, God," she said, her hand covering her mouth. "The sickness wasn't a pestilence, was it? I think I know where the Harpers are."

"I think I'm gonna be sick," Swift said, hunching over, his hands resting on his knees. He retched, spitting onto the grass in front of him.

The crowds moved away from them; their whispers turned to mutterings of disgust. Annie felt her knees weaken under her and she quickly dropped to her haunches before she collapsed completely, head low to stop herself from fainting. Minutes passed and neither of them moved. The grass, inches from Annie's face, smelt sweet and new and fresh; she drew in great lungfuls, trying to quell the nausea. She had to get up. She had to know for sure.

"Swift." Annie grabbed his arm, hauling him to his feet. "We need to go and check."

He straightened, nodding, his face a shiny putty. They walked to the edge of the green, aware that the chatter around them had quietened, eyes boring into the backs of their heads. When they were out of sight of the villagers, they ran. Up the tarmac, back towards the church, towards the cottage, and stopping at the entrance to the field on the other side of the lane. The water tower loomed over them like a giant. Weeds crept up its sides, wrapping around the base of the rusty fence protecting the villagers from harm. Annie jumped the gate to the field and ran towards the structure. The fence was only waist high, battened down in places where people, probably teens, had jumped the barbed wire. Swift put his coat across the spikes, and they climbed over it.

The tower was crumbling in places, the brickwork worn away by years of cold winds and rain. Up here on the hill it was open to all the elements, but that wasn't what had done the damage. They rounded the building, finding a narrow ladder at the back, and started to climb.

"What was it that gave it away?" Swift asked, as he placed hand over hand to get to the top.

"The bottled water," Annie said, slipping on a rusty rung and grabbing hold with white knuckles. "Just after the Harpers went missing, the whole village got sick."

"And the vicar and Alf only drink bottled water," Swift added.

Annie's breathing became laboured the higher she climbed, and she stopped talking to concentrate on reaching a platform above her. It stretched the entire circumference of the tower, a few feet from the top.

Swift pushed open a trapdoor and lifted himself up, lowering a hand to help Annie. This high, and with little protection save a small metal fence, the wind buffeted them against the top of the tower.

"Look," Annie pointed to a small door, gun metal, flush against the brickwork.

They edged carefully around the platform towards the door and Swift pushed. Surprisingly the door swung open without a complaint and the smell of damp hit Annie as she peered in. Inside the tower was dark, the sound of water below echoing between the walls. Around the inside edge was another platform giving way to a sheer drop down. Two strands of flimsy chain link looped around it; it looked more like a trip hazard than a safety feature.

"Watch your step," Swift said, treading over the threshold and into the tower.

Annie grabbed a piece of paper from her pocket to use as a door stop, not wanting to be trapped inside the tower, unable to open the door from the inside. It was the photograph she'd taken from the cellar on the first day. The Harpers at their car.

"Swift, look," she said, showing it to her boss in the dim light of the door.

"The Harpers?" he asked, tilting the picture to get a better view.

"Not the Harpers," Annie pointed to the vehicle behind them.

"The car?" Swift said, looking back up at Annie, his brows knotted. "That's the car we saw in Alf's yard."

Annie nodded, a sickness sinking to the bottom of her stomach. She folded the paper and tucked it into the hinge of the door, stepping inside as it swung shut behind her. They were plunged into darkness. Fumbling around for her phone, the sound of clapping stopped her in her tracks.

Clap. Clap. Clap.

Long, slow. She felt like she was in a nightmare. As her eyes adjusted to the darkness, over the other side of the tower, Annie could see Alf, hitting his hands together with an ear aching force. At his feet was the vicar.

"I told you to leave," the vicar said, and Alf gave her a shove with his foot.

"Shut up," he spat. "You've done enough damage already."

The vicar whimpered and shuffled backwards, away from the edge of the platform.

"Alf," Swift said, holding up his warrant badge. "Police. You need to step away from the edge and let the vicar go."

Alf gave a course laugh.

"You think I care who you are?" he shouted, his angry words banging off the walls.

"It was an accident, Freddy," the vicar said, hunched on the floor. "Give it up now, God forgives you."

"I SAID SHUT UP."

The vicar curled up as small as she could, Annie could see her face was bloodied, a red trickle running down her forehead.

Alf paced back and forth at her feet, the chain fence rattling as his trousers brushed against it. One push from the vicar and Alf would fall to his death to lie alongside the Harpers in the freezing cold water.

"What happened, Alf?" Annie asked. "Why did you put them in here? Why couldn't you give them a proper buried spot? Especially the son, he was only a baby."

Alf's hands gripped each other so tightly Annie could see the strength in his forearms. He must have dragged the vicar up here, there was no way she could have climbed that ladder. He was strong for a man so old. Yet, from across the tower, Annie could see no wrinkles on his face and, in the darkness, his hair could have been any colour, shaving years off his age. He looked fifty, at most.

"I didn't touch that baby," he said, dark eyes on Annie. "If he hadn't been there, none of this would have happened. But I didn't harm a hair on his head."

Annie could feel Swift move behind her, slowly, gently, keeping in the shadows. She didn't like what he was doing, but they had no other choice. Annie found her phone and switched on her torch, aiming it across the water, away from where Swift was creeping around the edge.

"So where are the Harpers?" she asked, not only curious, but also trying to draw Alf's attention away. "What happened to the Harper baby?"

"It's over, Freddy," the vicar said, softly. "Why don't you confess in front of someone else? Take this burden away from me. Let me live the rest of my years without this guilt hanging over my head."

She gave a great, heaving cough, spitting up blood onto the concrete at her feet. Alf faltered in his step, looking down at the vicar and back across the water at Annie.

"I couldn't get caught again," he said, casting his eyes downwards. "I'd already been to juvie for theft and joyriding, and I'd just turned eighteen so I was looking at a real sentence."

So Alf *was* only in his fifties. Life hadn't been kind to him, and Annie suspected he used that to his advantage.

"What would you have been caught doing?" Annie asked.

"It wasn't my fault," Alf started. "The Harpers left the keys in the ignition. I was just waking past. They had this brand-new Ford, all shiny it was. So I got in. I was only going to take it for a spin up and down the lane, nothing awful." He took a shuddering breath. "Only, when I got going I realised the kid were in the back, didn't I? And the Harpers realised too. I was taking it back. I was going to leave it where I found it. Kid an' all. It were screaming at me. Have you ever heard a screaming baby? It's all I could do to concentrate. And I only looked behind me for a second, trying to shut the little beggar up. It wasn't my fault."

"You hit them?" Annie asked, imagining how awful that baby must have felt as the car crashed into its petrified parents.

"They'd run out into the road, what was I supposed to do?"

"Stop? Call an ambulance?" Annie turned to the vicar. "You knew about this?"

The old woman crossed herself and nodded.

"I heard the crash," she said, sadly. "I was in the church at the time. When I came out… they were… they were already dead. God rest their souls. That young lad was screaming so loudly. I couldn't stand it."

"He'd just witnessed the death of his parents," Annie said. "What do you expect?"

"He was months old," the vicar shouted. "He didn't know what was going on."

"But you did." Annie felt like she was talking to a brick wall. "What did you do to him?"

"I told Freddie to get rid of the bodies." Her face grew slack. "Said to dump them up here because they'd never find them. It was only too late I realised he'd put them in the water."

"And the baby?" Annie cried.

"I took that child and made sure he was safe."

"You took him away from a trauma and hid him?" Annie spat. "Did that make you feel better about concealing a crime?"

"He went to a good, loving, God fearing family." Her voice grew louder. "They cared for him, and he grew to be a fine young man. A doctor. Only, he came back, not that long ago, he started asking questions about your sister."

Annie felt her world tilt on its axis.

"Harry Metcalf?" Her voice shook as she said the name of the man who'd tried to take her life.

"Yes," the vicar replied, unaware. "That's why I sent your sister away, why I turned the village against her.

233

She would have ruined it for Alfie and me. I don't know if Harry knew about his past, but I wasn't willing to wait and find out."

Annie wanted to tell the vicar that Harry hadn't been after revealing his past, he'd been after *her*, but the world was spinning too fast to grasp onto the facts. No wonder Harry had been traumatised, not only did he have the murder suicide of his adopted mother and sister to deal with, he'd been exposed to serious trauma at a very young age. She almost felt sorry for him. Almost.

"Why didn't you just call the police?" Annie said, wearily, directing the question at the vicar, but Alf was the one who answered.

"She wanted them poking around about as much as I did," he said, his voice dripping with malice.

And Annie realised then, why the vicar had looked so familiar when they'd first met. She looked like Alf.

"She's your mum?" she said, not really a question at all.

"Didn't want her darling boy going to jail, now, did she?" Alf started pacing again. "She'd get removed from the village, no one wants a vicar with a crap family tainting their parish."

Swift was nearly there, slowly shuffling around towards the vicar and her son.

"So you started the rumours about the witch?" Annie asked.

Alf laughed again.

"No," he said, chuckling. "That was those idiots Lewis and Isla. Lewis' family business was going under and no amount of fraud from him was going to rescue it. They came up with this plan to exploit the missing family and old Maddie was the best scape-goat they could have wished for. The rest of the village getting sick from the water contamination made me feel terrible, but then they linked that to the sacrifice too. What could I do? People had started to come here to see the *cursed place.* I was worried they'd find the bodies. But no one came for me, and soon the village was thriving. Madeleine may have left because she was getting too much attention, but she's happy in a retirement home in Cumbria. And, apart from that, what I did made this village what it is today. We were sinking like all the other mining towns and look at us now. We just want to live peace-fully and happily."

"So did the Harpers," Annie said, disbelieving that Alf could see what he'd done as a positive thing. "Both the parents and that poor child."

"Then they really did make the ultimate sacrifice," Alf said, his gaze fixed on Annie. "And I'm not going to let you ruin what we've made here." He turned to Swift. "That includes you, hot shot police officer. You can come and catch me if you like, but there's no way you'll get out of this village alive. Look."

Alf indicated to the door Annie had propped open. Swift stopped where he was, his fists balled.

"Go on," he said to Annie. "What's he talking about?"

Annie shuffled back to the door and pushed it open.

"These villagers knew there was something up with you." Alf was walking away from Swift and around towards Annie. "They believe. Apart from the school who benefits as much as I do from the rumour, and Isla and Lewis, everyone else believes the witch is real. I told them you were angering the witch. I cannot be held responsible for how they react."

Annie couldn't speak. She looked down at the field under the tower, to the crowd gathering there. They held pitchforks, flamed torches, and some even had shotguns strapped to their shoulders.

"Swift," Annie said, as one man below pointed up to her. "We have a problem."

TWENTY-THREE

THE MOB HAD FOUND THEM.

And they were angry.

Smoke rose from the torches, acrid and thick. Annie coughed, ducking her head back inside the water tower and pushing the door to.

"How do they know where we are?" Annie shouted, wiping her sweat on her top lip with the back of her hand.

Alf held up his mobile phone, shrugging.

"They deserve to keep believing," he said, edging towards Annie.

"Don't move," Swift shouted. Annie saw him in her peripheral vision edging back to her as quickly as he dared.

Across the gaping void, the vicar sat hunched into herself, rocking gently, any noise coming from her was drowned out by the chanting from outside the tower.

"Why couldn't you just heed the warnings and leave Ethlake?" Alf said, wearily. "You'd be halfway back to Norfolk by now, safely tucking into a Little Chef breakfast."

He looked past Annie and his wide-mouthed grin stretched even further.

"I needed to know the truth about my sister," Annie said. "I couldn't leave here without hearing what happened. I knew you were all lying about knowing her. I just couldn't work out why. And now I know, I have to find her. Where did she go?"

Alf stepped up to Annie, prodding her painfully in the chest with a sharp finger. She held her ground, though fear was threatening to buckle her knees out from under her.

"Your bloody sister asked as many questions as you two." Alf prodded her again, accentuating every word with his pointed fingers. "I didn't know mother had sent her away and goodness knows where she is now, but if it's been that long since you saw her, maybe take the hint?"

Up close it was obvious that Alf wasn't an old man. His skin, though weathered, was wrinkled with anger and not age. Under the facade was someone strong enough to take her over the edge. He pulled open the door, the roaring of the angry villagers below like something from the Middle Ages. It was a witch hunt. Whether they believed or not.

"People of Ethlake," Alf shouted down to them, stepping out of the tower onto the platform, his arms raised like a prophet. "These outsiders are here to break our pact. They've angered the witch. You can see that from the way she's cast a shadow over our village today."

Annie felt warmth behind her, a safe hand on her shoulder.

"We need to get out of here," Swift whispered.

But there was no way to go except towards the angry mob and the man riling them. At the head of the crowd Annie could see Gerry, nodding frantically, a long broom in his hands. The fear on his face as apparent as it had been back in the witch's house. He believed. And fear could make even the sanest of people carry out acts of atrocity.

Alf stepped back inside and before she knew what was happened, he'd grabbed Annie's collar and was dragging her out the door. She scratched at his fingers, tried to prise them off her coat. Her feet dragged precariously close to the low railing outside.

"This," Alf shouted, "is why our village will not prosper next year. Why we've had to work extra hard this week to settle the witch. Do we want this? Do we want people like *her* coming here and ruining our lives?"

No!

The mob was moving as one, rocking gently back and forth. Annie knew that down there, people would be getting crushed between those around them, adding to their frenetic panic. At the back of the crowd, she could just make out the four hens, waving their glasses in glee. They must think that this is all part of the performance. Alf squeezed his hand and Annie felt her throat constrict.

"Come any closer and I'll drop her," Alf hissed, and Swift backed off, his arms raised in surrender.

The madman dragged Annie to the edge of the platform, the rail bashed painfully against her knee. Panic was building in her, her eyes felt as though they would pop right out of her skull, her face felt puce. She grappled at his hands, digging her nails into the soft part of flesh where his thumb met his forefinger.

Alf cried out, loosening his grip enough for Annie to catch breath. She drew long, deep lungfuls of oxygen, her head spinning.

"You're not going to get away with this," Swift shouted from inside the tower.

"No?" Alf shouted back, his eyes wide, darting around inside his head. "What are you going to do? Arrest me? Carry me down the ladder?"

"No," Swift cried, and Annie could hear the pain in his voice. "Something a hell of a lot worse. Look."

Annie felt movement as Alf twisted to see what Swift meant. His grip loosened, she felt herself fall forwards, the crowd below rush up to meet her. Reaching out a hand, she wildly groped for something to grip onto, to stop her from falling, Annie squeezed her eyes shut, realisation hitting her. Thoughts of her mother, her sister, Swift came full throttle into her head, skitting around like wasps. Her fingers brushed the metal rails, quickly she grabbed, ignoring the searing pain across her palms. Her body slammed against the brickwork, knocking the breath out of her lungs and the scream from her lips.

The crowd below grew quiet, their chants losing the momentum, the chorus stuttered and out of sync. Annie's arm throbbed. She swung herself around and reached up with the other hand, gasps of fright filtering up from below. Over the railing, Alf was edging back into the tower, arms outstretched as though feeling the way. She hauled herself up and back onto the platform, her heart beating in her mouth. She saw Swift and the bile rose in her throat.

Over the void, across the gaping black hole he stood. Trapped in his arms was the vicar, so close to the edge that her feet were on tip toes, scuffing dust into the water way below.

"Swift?" Annie coaxed. "What are you doing?"

"Saving your life, Annie," he said, his eyes not leaving Alf.

The vicar gave a whimper as Swift pushed her closer to the edge.

"Don't come any closer, Alfred," he said. "You're not the only one who can manipulate others because humans feel love. At the end of the day, our weaknesses only expose that we're good people really."

If her heart beat any faster, Annie thought it would force her into the water.

"I...," Alf stumbled over his feet, gripping the wall to stop himself falling forwards. "Mum? Are you okay?"

His voice was like a child's.

"Swift?" Annie took the opposite direction to Alf, walking towards where Swift was holding the vicar captive. "It's okay, I'm alright now. You can let her go."

Alf was trembling, his hands white where he pressed them against the wall.

"Annie," Swift said, the emotion void from his words. "Do you remember the church house where we found Tim Barclay?"

Swift was talking about the very first case they worked together, a house he'd broken into without a warrant. She nodded.

"And Headmaster Haversham's office?" he went on.

Another time Swift had bent the rules. She nodded again.

"And when you came to stay at mine after your accident? And what happened with Harry."

Annie sucked in a breath. She'd thought too much about Harry already today. What was Swift implying? She'd broken the rules then too. She'd killed a man in self-defence. Is that what Swift meant? Was he going to kill the vicar to make sure she was safe? Annie didn't want any more blood on her hands. This was a defenceless old woman, not a crazed psychopath trying to kill her. She shook her head this time.

"Swift, no, you don't need to," she cried, edging towards him.

"Each of those events," he said, and Annie could see him tightening his grip on the vicar's cassock. "There was something I asked of you. Can you remember what it was?"

Annie shook her head harder. She didn't know what he meant. Reaching out a hand, she placed it gently on his arm, feeling the muscle tense beneath her fingers.

"Swift, we can go now," she said, her voice shaking. "We can leave. The mob is dying down, they don't know what they're doing anymore. We'll be okay."

As she spoke the words, the door of the tower burst open. Lewis stood in the bright sun, a silhouette of a man, the outline of his shotgun clear to see.

"Lewis," Alf cried. "Stop."

"No Alf," Lewis shouted, his hard words echoing around the tower. "They're going to ruin what we've built. I didn't work my arse off after taking the pub over from my family for it to be torn apart by two nosey idiots wanting to play at being heroes."

He raised the gun to his eye.

"What about getting some sort of closure for the Harpers?" Annie cried.

Lewis scoffed. "Those gits? They ran off and left us when the going got tough. Who cares about them?"

So no-one knew about the accident except Alf and his mum?

"I was wrong," Alf cried. "Please Lewis, they're going to take the vicar down with them if you shoot."

"She's getting old anyway." Lewis aimed the shotgun directly at Swift's chest, avoiding Annie and the vicar would be impossible.

"What about ricochet?" Annie gasped, clutching at straws.

Lewis shrugged. "I can shut the door."

Alf burst into tears, knowing he'd not be able to escape from any diverted bullets.

"Annie." Swift was insistent. "What was it I asked of you?"

Tears tracked down her cheeks, flying from her face as she kept shaking her head.

"I don't know, Swift." She was sobbing, her eyes blurred with tears. "I'm sorry. I don't know."

He took a deep breath and grabbed at Annie's hand.

"To trust me," he said.

And he jumped, taking the vicar and Annie with him.

TWENTY-FOUR

THEY FELL.

Dropping like stones. Annie wheeled her free arm, kicking with her legs. The drop was long. And when they plunged into the water it was as cold as ice.

What was Swift thinking? Surely he didn't mean to kill the old woman?

Annie's whole body froze in fear, her lungs drew in air as her diaphragm constricted with the temperature of the water. Then her head fell below the surface, blocking out the world with a stillness that was freeing. She felt herself falling, sucked down by the weight of her clothes. A calmness fell over her as she drifted down, down, down. Then she was hit with an all-consuming panic.

With both hands free, she kicked and pushed through the water as hard as she could. Her jeans heavy and a counterweight. Her coat was soaking up the water. Shrugging out of it, Annie gave one final push, her lungs burning.

She surfaced, gulping in air as fast as she could. Her teeth chattered loudly. Above her, she could hear the anguished cries of Alf, the angry shouts of Lewis. She was tired. Too tired to stay afloat. Under her feet she could feel the bones of the Harpers, grabbing at her ankles. Even if it was just in her head, the fear was making her sink.

What was she going to do? How were they going to get out? Where was Swift? She felt her head duck under the water again, coughing and spluttering as she surfaced. A hand gripped her shoulder, moving painfully down her arm and pulling. Rough brick scuffed against her bare arms, cutting into her skin. But she was out of the water.

Panting, Annie felt around with her fingers, the darkness this far down the tower was an all-consuming blackness. A small brick lip protruded out of the water, just wide enough for her to perch on. Her fingers brushed material, long, heavy. *The vicar?*

"This way." The old woman's voice was gravelly, whispering as quietly as she could.

Swift was on her other side, his hand finding hers and squeezing gently. *It's okay.*

Annie shuffled around the ledge until the vicar came to a stop.

"My fingers are too cold," the vicar whispered. And she felt her own hands enveloped by the vicar's, lifted and placed on a metal handle.

"What is this?" she whispered back.

"Safety door," the vicar said quietly. "It's a hatch. Pull it."

Annie wrapped her fingers around the handle and pulled. The sound of metal grating on metal bounced off the walls. Annie hoped that the men at the top of the tower were already on their way down the ladder or they'd know something was happening down here.

The hatch fell down, bright sunlight flooded the tower. Annie could see the vicar's face, her blue lips shivering. On her other side, Swift hauled himself to a stand, holding a hand out for her.

"You two go first," the vicar said. "There's a small ladder to the floor. We're on the other side to the entrance, so if you hurry, you may be able to get out of here before they realise what's happening."

"But vicar," Annie said, holding her hand out to help the old woman up and out of the hatch. "You're freezing. You need to go first, to warm up."

The old woman batted Annie's hand away.

"If the lord wants me to live," she said, coughing. "I will live. Now go."

Annie could hear the sounds of the crowd growing. She climbed onto the metal hatch, feet first to the ladder.

"Thank you," she said. "I hope you'll be okay."

The vicar lowered her eyes.

"I'm sorry."

Annie found the rung with her feet, stepping down into the warm sun. She climbed down to the weeds below, searching around for any signs they'd been seen. The coast was clear. She could see the gap in the fence where they'd climbed over it, Swift's coat still dampening the barbed wire.

"Go, quickly," Swift hissed as he jumped to the ground.

She grabbed his hand and they ran. Over the weeds. Away from the water tower. Away from the voices as they shouted their escape. They jumped over the wire fence. Swift gave no notion to rescue his jacket. And they fled across the lane to the cottage and their waiting car.

"Quick," Annie yelled as Swift fumbled for the car keys. "They're coming."

Behind them, Annie could see Lewis and Isla heading the crowd. His gun raised, his face puce with anger. She ducked as a shot ran out into the sky. Even as the crows started to falter, the four hens were jumping up and down in glee, oblivious to the reality, drawn in by the acts that everyone in this god-awful village were playing. This was what they wanted, the villagers of Ethlake, a reality of their own not governed by real life. And they were willing to stop at nothing to get it.

The car door clunked as Swift unlocked it and Annie was inside in an instant, pulling the door shut behind her and ducking under the glove box.

"Get down," Swift yelled as he hit the ignition and pulled the car out of the drive.

Another gun shot burst across the bonnet, scraping paint as it went. Annie squealed and hid under her arms as they bumped down the lane towards the green. Sirens split the air and Annie came out from her hiding place. Two police cars raced up the hill towards them, Swift pulled over to let them past, stopping only long enough for Annie to see Alf and his mum burst out from the trees.

"How did you know?" Annie asked Swift as they turned a corner and left the village. "That we'd be okay if we jumped?"

Swift dropped his speed, glancing in the rear-view mirror. He hit the heater and a blast of hot air covered

Annie like a blanket. She hadn't realised how much she was shivering sitting there in wet clothes.

"The vicar knew," he said, his teeth chattering too. "She told me it was the only way out. She knew the danger we were in and she was willing to sacrifice herself to help us."

Annie felt a tug of sadness in her chest. Her whole adult life, the vicar had kept a secret in order to save her son. Wouldn't any other parent do the same?

"Do you think she'll be arrested? Will they find the bones after all this time?" she asked, pulling off her t-shirt and groping around on the back seats for a blanket.

"They both will," Swift replied, nodding. "And Lewis too, I imagine. For firing a dangerous weapon at the very least."

"Don't we need to stay?" Annie asked. "So they can take our statements?"

Swift laughed. "Probably. But I'm not turning around now, not after the day we've just had. We'll ring them when we get back to Norfolk."

"How did they know? The police, I mean."

"When Alf had you dangling out there on that ledge I called for back up." Swift rubbed the back of his neck, his cheeks growing pink.

Annie remembered what he'd told Alf, about his weakness being love. Had Swift meant her? Was Annie Swift's weakness? It wasn't the right time to ask, so Annie let the idea slip away with the hills.

"I can't believe Harry was the missing Harper baby," she said, watching the fields fly by outside the window. "It kind of makes me understand more about how he turned out as an adult."

"It is strange that your sister ended up in the same place that Harry disappeared," Swift replied, winding his window down and letting in a warm blast of air. "Like a circle of life, except not life. But nothing will make me understand that man."

They trundled down the lane. Past the farm where they'd been trapped by cows, past the signs to the South, past the hills as they flattened to fields and sped by in swathes of green and yellow. Soon they were back on the motorway and well on their way back to Norfolk.

Annie felt her jeans tightening around her legs as they dried. They were itching and uncomfortable. She reached around, not quite able to reach her suitcase. Shrugging, she unzipped her trousers anyway, hoiking them down over her legs with difficulty. As she was trying to pull them over her ankles, her phone fell to the car floor with a thud.

"Urgh," she said, picking it up and checking it over. "How waterproof do you think this is?"

Holding it up to the light, Annie laughed as a torrent of water fell from the charging point.

"As waterproof as my pants," Swift said, laughing himself. "Which is not very, and they're chaffing."

Annie couldn't help another bubble of laughter burst from her mouth.

"Shall we stop at the services and get changed?" she asked, something else on the floor catching her eye.

"Good idea," Swift replied.

Bending down to pick it up, Annie turned it over in her hands. A piece of paper that had been in her pocket with her phone. Knowing she hadn't put it there, Annie started to unravel it. Carefully, as the paper was soaked with water too, she peeled in open where it had been folded in quarters. Half, then half again, she undid it. Something had been typed, a mobile number from the looks of it. The typeface had withstood the drenching. As had the headed print at the top of the page. It was church paper.

"What's that?" Swift asked, indicating to turn off on a slip road towards a service station.

Annie thought back to the village green, before the chaos, before Alf had come for his mum. When the vicar had been talking to them, Annie had felt a bump against her side. Had the vicar planted this in her pocket? What was it? She looked again at the number, blue ink above it soaked into the paper like a water-colour painting. Then, all at once, Annie knew what it was and her heart soared.

"I think it's my sister's mobile number," she said, clutching at the paper with trembling fingers. "I think the vicar gave me this as an apology."

"Mim's number?" Swift said, peering over at the paper in Annie's hand. "You think it still works?"

Annie's voice stuck in her throat, thick with emotion.

"There's only one way to find out."

Swift pulled into a space at the back of the carpark and killed the engine. He unstuck himself from his chair and turned to Annie.

"I'm right here for you," he said, putting a cold hand on hers. "Whatever you decide to do."

"But my phone," she said, half relieved. "I'll have to wait until we get back."

Swift shook his head, leaning over her and popping the glove box. An old Nokia lay on top of the service manual.

"In case of wifi emergencies," he said, shrugging.

With shaking hands, wrapped in a blanket in her underwear, Annie pulled the phone out and held down

254

the power button. It flashed to life, singing the tune she remembered so well from her teens. The air in the car stilled, as though waiting with her. Punching in the number, unable to draw breath, Annie held the phone to her ear and listened as it connected.

It rang, and Annie's heart stopped as the peels stopped.

"Hello, Miriam O'Malley," a young voice said.

Annie felt her eyes fill with tears, blinking them away.

"Mim," she said, her voice shaking. "Mim? It's me. It's Annie, your sister."

Read on to find out what happens to Annie and Swift in the next instalment of their adventure…

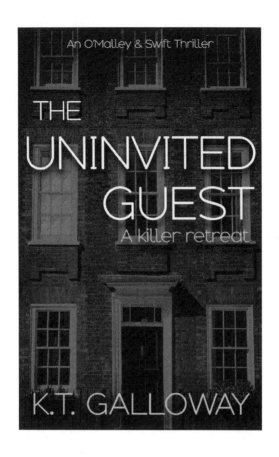

Annie O'Malley & DI Swift return in The Uninvited Guest.

BLURB

Welcome to Paradise Grove, a killer retreat...

Back in Norfolk and back to work, Annie O'Malley and DI Swift are called to an isolated seaside village and the exclusive Paradise Grove Spa.

Renowned for its peace and tranquility, the spa and its staff offer the chance to relax and recuperate in a discrete private setting on its own causeway. So when a dead body turns up in one of the rooms with no clue to who he is or how he got there, suspicion falls on the secretive group of guests.

Cut off by the encroaching tidal swell, O'Malley and Swift find themselves in a race against time to eliminate the suspects before the killer eliminates them.

The fifth instalment in the O'Malley and Swift series that readers are calling 'atmospheric and authentic.

Buy now
KTgallowaybooks.com

THANK YOU!

Thank you so much for reading The House of Secrets. It's hard for me to put into words how much I appreciate my readers. If you enjoyed The House of Secrets, I would greatly appreciate it if you took the time to review on Amazon, Goodreads, or Bookbub.

You can also find me at ktgallowaybooks.com

ALSO BY K.T. GALLOWAY

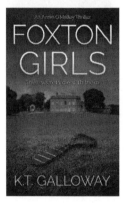

An Annie O'Malley Thriller

WE ALL FALL DOWN

Ring a ring o' roses

K.T. GALLOWAY

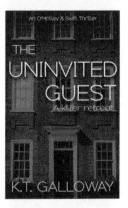

An O'Malley & Swift Thriller

THE UNINVITED GUEST

A killer retreat

K.T. GALLOWAY

An O'Malley & Swift Thriller

DEADLY GAMES

K.T. GALLOWAY

Printed in Great Britain
by Amazon